Past Praise for Misty M. Beller

"Misty Beller is one of the most amazing and enticing story-tellers that Bethany House has to offer. I love reading her books and enjoy her ability to bring the characters to life. I encourage my readers to give her a try."

—Tracie Peterson, bestselling author of over 100 books, including the PICTURES OF THE HEART and THE JEWELS OF KALISPELL series

"Misty Beller writes about protection—of family, of neighbors, of all God's creatures and souls. *Rocky Mountain Promise* keeps the faith in continuing the adventures of the Collins sisters, their connection to the Wyoming landscape, and their lives navigating the fur trapping era's demands on both men and women, on hearts and minds. Lorelei takes center stage in this story that should encourage readers of the frontier and readers of faith. More than a romance, it's a story of helping and hope. Another bestseller for sure."

—Jane Kirkpatrick, award-winning author of *Beneath the Bending Skies*

Rocky Mountain Journey

SISTERS of the ROCKIES • 3

ROCKY MOUNTAIN JOURNEY

MISTY M. BELLER

BETHANYHOUSE

a division of Baker Publishing Group
Minneapolis, Minnesota

© 2024 by Misty M. Beller

Published by Bethany House Publishers
Minneapolis, Minnesota
BethanyHouse.com

Bethany House Publishers is a division of
Baker Publishing Group, Grand Rapids, Michigan

Printed in the United States of America

Library of Congress Cataloging-in-Publication Data
Names: Beller, Misty M., author.
Title: Rocky Mountain Journey / Misty M. Beller.
Description: Minneapolis, Minnesota : Bethany House, a division of Baker Publishing
    Group, 2024. | Series: Sisters of the Rockies ; 3
Identifiers: LCCN 2023055263 | ISBN 9780764241550 (paperback) | ISBN
    9780764243219 (casebound) | ISBN 9781493446629 (e-book)
Subjects: LCGFT: Christian fiction. | Romance fiction. | Novels.
Classification: LCC PS3602.E45755 R57 2024 | DDC 813/.6—dc23/eng/20231208
LC record available at https://lccn.loc.gov/2023055263

Scripture quotations are from the King James Version of the Bible.

Cover design by Dan Thornberg, Design Source Creative Services
Cover images from Shutterstock

Author is represented by Books & Such Literary Agency.

Baker Publishing Group publications use paper produced from sustainable forestry practices and postconsumer waste whenever possible.

24 25 26 27 28 29 30   7 6 5 4 3 2 1

To my sweet daughter Leah Faith,
my inspiration and namesake for Faith's character.
I love your tenacity, your wit, and your charm.
I knew before you were born
that God made you for great things!

He that dwelleth in the secret place of the Most High
shall abide under the shadow of the Almighty.
I will say of the LORD, He is my refuge and my
fortress: my God; in him will I trust.

Psalm 91:1–2

ONE

July 1839
Green River Valley (Future Wyoming)

The stallion's muscles coiled beneath Faith as the massive animal prepared to rear. But she wouldn't let him throw her—wouldn't lose control. Exhaling slowly to keep her own body from tensing, she crooned, "Easy, boy."

She had a job to do, and she would not fail. The sooner she finished this horse's training, the sooner the family could continue their search for Steps Right. She gripped the reins tighter and pressed her weight deeper into her heels. If he shied sideways or lunged forward into a bucking fit, she'd be ready. This stallion's determination and endurance were not to be underestimated. Those qualities would make him an excellent cavalry mount . . . *if* she trained him into a solid riding horse first. In this moment, she needed him to walk around the corral without attempting to throw her.

The stallion's front legs lifted off the ground, and her lungs froze as she steadied herself. Then he landed on his toes. He'd risen just enough to threaten a full rear.

"Walk on." She nudged him forward with her heels. No matter what, she couldn't let him feel the fear that gnawed at the edges of her confidence. Too much depended on her finishing this animal's training.

He settled into a flat-footed walk for a half-dozen steps, then his muscles coiled again. The warning came only a heartbeat before his front legs rose up in a full rear.

Her heart surged, and she leaned forward to keep their balance upright, loosening her reins and flicking the ends on his shoulder.

"Walk on!" The words came out more as a roar than a shout, but her tone accomplished her goal.

The stallion dropped his front legs to the ground.

She dug her heels into his sides and said again, "Walk on."

He obeyed, jigging forward a few steps, then finally settled into a calmer walk. She worked to make her body relax again. Horses fed on tension. If he sensed it within her, he'd act out more.

"That's enough for today, Faith." Rosemary's commanding voice sounded across the yard from the front porch of their cabin. "End on a good note, then come help me with the food."

Not now. She was just making headway. Surely Rosie understood she needed to take advantage of every moment when the stallion would cooperate.

Faith let her focus dart toward her sister for only a second before returning to the horse's ears, which were now pointed firmly in the direction he stared—toward Rosie and their one-year-old niece, Bertie, who was propped on her hip. Distracted like that, he could startle easily.

Faith shook her head and kept her tone pleasant for the

horse's sake. "I think he needs more time cantering to wear off his extra energy. He's still not focusing."

"Save it for tomorrow. I need you in the house."

She grunted her frustration but kept her reins loose so the horse didn't feed off the emotion. Didn't Rosie understand how important it was for her to work the stallion when she could make headway? Why were her plans and goals always the ones that had to be delayed to help the rest of the family? It wasn't as if she was being selfish in riding this stallion. Training the younger horses was one of her main jobs on this ranch that she and her sisters owned together. They were supposed to be running it as equals. But she was the only one who bent to the others' needs.

She halted the stallion and slid to the ground, then led him toward the corral gate, using her sleeve to wipe the sweat running down her temple. July in this mountain country wasn't as hot and humid as it had been back in Virginia, but an afternoon working with the horses in the piercing sun had stripped the strength from her weary body.

As she led the horse toward the barn, a little voice called from the cabin. "Da da da da da." Bertie stood at the top of the porch steps, her pudgy arms waving.

Just the sight of her niece's sweet smile lifted a bit of the exhaustion from Faith's shoulders. Bertie had been walking since Christmas but still always seemed on the verge of losing her balance—and often did.

She tied the stallion to a hitching rail, then strode across the yard toward her niece. She could unsaddle the animal in a moment, but right now she needed the joy that came when she played with Bertie—and to make sure she didn't tumble down those steps.

She clomped up the porch stairs, then bent low and scooped up her niece. "Hello there, my sweet one. Can you say 'Auntie Faith'?"

Bertie grinned, her round cheeks appling as she revealed a mouth full of mostly new teeth. "Da da da." That was the sound the child made most. Perhaps because her "dada" Riley doted on her so.

Faith chuckled, then gave the girl a quick tickle in her belly. "Where's your mama and Aunt Rosie?" Rosie had disappeared inside when Faith approached the porch, probably rushing to stir something on the cookstove.

Rosie had been working hard to prepare a spread of food for the celebration meal to be held that evening—a special farewell supper for their missionary friends who'd been visiting for the past week. Goes Ahead, Elise, and their children would leave tomorrow to continue traveling through the mountains, working with the tribes and sharing their faith.

"I'm right here," Rosie said from inside the cabin. "Keep Bertie outside, though, so she doesn't wake Juniper."

Faith turned back to her niece. "Is your mama sleeping?" Being in the family way again sapped the strength from Juniper.

Though her and Riley's cabin on the ranch wasn't far, her sister caught a nap in Rosemary's room when she could, if she and Bertie were helping with something in the main house.

"Mama." The child gave a slow nod, the motion bouncing her brown curls.

"That's good." Juniper seemed to be faring better this time around, not casting up her accounts every few hours, as she had done with Bertie. Still, June carried dark shadows under her eyes, and her face had swelled early.

Keep her and the babe safe, Lord. Please.

Lorelei too.

So much had happened since they'd traveled to this land. The other of their sisters who'd recently married had just announced last week that she and Tanner were expecting. So far, she'd shown no signs of sickness, only a constant glow that made her beam all the time.

Bertie rested a hand on Faith's cheek, then seemed to catch herself. She pulled her hand back and ducked her chin, peering up at Faith with a shy smile that nearly melted Faith's heart.

She pulled her close and gave her a tight squeeze. "I love you, Bertie girl."

Bertie squirmed, as she often did when constrained, and Faith released her, adjusting the girl on her hip.

"Owie." Bertie reached into the pocket on her pinafore, as though something had poked her during the hug.

"Did I squeeze you too tight? I'm sorry."

Bertie pulled out something that flashed in the sunlight.

"What is that?" Faith squinted against the sparkle. Whatever it was, the child probably shouldn't be playing with it. Had she absconded with Rosemary's locket that had been passed down from their mother? At least Rosie had something of Mama's.

Faith pushed down the old familiar twinge of jealousy. The one thing *she'd* had to remember Mama by—the stones the two of them had collected together—had been lost when they moved from their Virginia ranch to Richmond after Mama's death.

The child tucked her hand behind her back, her lips pinched, likely knowing she wasn't supposed to have the item.

Faith reached for Bertie's arm. "I'll bet Aunt Rosie wouldn't want you to have that." She kept her voice light and pleasant. "Can you give it to Auntie Faith?"

When she pried Bertie's hand from behind her, the girl finally raised the trinket with her precious grin. "Da."

Faith's breath caught as she focused on the necklace in her niece's hand. This wasn't the locket on its thin gold chain. She reached for the blue crystal beads, but when Bertie tried to pull them away, Faith caught her wrist instead. "No, ma'am."

Bertie's face pinched, and she made a fussing sound, so Faith eased her grip. "You can't play with these, honey. They're very special." She used her other hand to pry the child's fingers open and slip the strand out of her hold.

With the necklace safe, she sighed and held it close to her chest. What would they have done if Bertie broke the cord and lost the beads? This keepsake could never have been replaced, not even if they somehow found the exact same type of beads and string to repair it. The meaning of this treasure would be lost.

Rosie poked her head through the doorway. "Stallion was good today?"

A flash of frustration gripped Faith. These beads were far more important than pleasantries. "Rosie." She held up the necklace. "Look what Bertie had in her pocket."

Rosemary squinted into the sunshine, then flashed a dismissive smile. "Ah. I was showing it to her yesterday. She must have seen which drawer I put it in."

Faith fought to keep anger from her tone. "Why would

you keep the beads where she could reach them? She might break the cord or the beads themselves, and the entire thing would be ruined. We'd never be able to accomplish what Papa asked." It was the entire reason the four of them had left everything and come west.

More than that, this strand had once saved their father's life. A rush of emotion surged through her, stinging her eyes. She turned away so her sister didn't see her childish display. None of the others cried for Papa anymore. It had been three years since his passing.

"Faith-ie."

She hated the way Rosie dragged her name into two syllables when she used that tone.

Her sister tipped her head like she was cajoling a selfish child. "She's not going to hurt the beads. And if she happened to break the cord, we could fix it. I don't think White Horse will mind. You know how much he loves Bertie."

What did White Horse have to do with this? Just because he was the son of the woman who'd saved their father's life more than a decade ago, and just because he'd been the only member of Steps Right's family they'd found when their father's final wish sent them west to find her, didn't mean he was *in charge* of the beads.

Or that he really had any say-so in what happened with them.

Papa had said to take the beads to Steps Right.

She could still see his dark eyes glistening as he'd begged her, his hand gripping hers. *"You're my courageous one, Faithie. You have to make sure this happens."*

Her sisters had been busy with other tasks in the room—Rosie talking with the doctor, Juniper at the basin pouring water for him to drink, and Lorelei pulling an extra blanket from the trunk.

Faith alone had stayed at his side. She'd feared those might be his final moments, though it seemed impossible to believe. But maybe God had kept her there, ensuring she was present for his final plea.

"You're my courageous one . . . make sure this happens."

And she would do what Papa asked. No matter the obstacles. No matter if her sisters moved on and forgot their important assignment.

When Faith and her sisters had first arrived in this wild territory, they'd searched quite a bit. They'd even found a cave where she'd stayed as well as a clue she'd left for White Horse that told him she was headed to a waterfall.

But since then, one unexpected obstacle after another had arisen. Then winter came with its massive snows that kept them mostly locked away in this valley, except for regular visits through the pass to see Tanner and Lorelei at the trading post. With spring came foaling season, which tied them to the ranch day and night as nearly a hundred mares gave birth. Rosemary had promised they'd begin searching again for Steps Right in the summer. Now it was nearly the end of July, and they still hadn't set out.

Bertie reached out for her aunt Rosie, and Faith handed the child over, then followed them into the cabin.

"Do you want to play with your blocks now?" Rosemary set the girl on the rug, and Bertie grabbed two wooden blocks with shapes painted on their sides. "We have to be quiet so your mama can sleep."

Rosie turned back to the kitchen area that took up one end of the cabin's main room, and Faith moved toward her so they could talk in soft tones. She forced a smile into her voice. "When can we go out and search the waterfalls?"

Rosie glanced her way with a frown, but Faith met it with a pleasant, expectant look. "I don't know. With Lorelei and Juniper both in the family way, now's not a good time for us to leave."

Frustration needled deeper, like a sharp bur under a heavy saddle, but she did her best not to let it show. "You said we could go in the summer. This is July. Definitely summer."

Rosie turned to load bread slices into a basket. "I said *maybe* summer. We can't go if we're needed here. Besides, White Horse said his mother's clue *might* mean she was taking refuge near a waterfall. We don't know for sure. He's always said she'll find a way to reach him if she needs anything."

Faith spun away from her vexing sister to wash her hands in the basin. "He might be wrong. What if Steps Right needs help and she doesn't have a way to send him a message? We have to find her. And waterfalls are the only clue we have. We won't be certain until we search them."

"And we will. As soon as we have time."

But would her sisters ever make time for their mission now that they'd settled in here on the ranch? The resolve inside Faith turned to steel. She had to be the strong one and carry out the commission Papa had given.

"And when will that time come? Next year? Ten years? This was the one thing Papa asked of us, Rosie. His *dying wish*. Find Steps Right and return the beads to her." She gripped the hand towel tighter, lest she say something she regretted. "Aren't you worried about her? White Horse saw those two braves from his old village leaving the trading post. He told me he thinks they might be searching for Steps Right. He looked worried too. What if they've already found her?" Panic welled in her chest like it did every time she thought of Steps Right's situation.

The elderly Peigan woman who possessed such a caring heart, who'd devoted her life to healing the sick and injured, unjustly sent away from her home and all she knew. She'd been hiding in these treacherous mountains for three years. What would those warriors do to her if they found her? Take her back to the village and make her endure some kind of trial or punishment?

A shiver slid through her, and she glared at Rosie. "I'm beginning to think you don't care. But I do." The burn of tears swept in fast. She was going to lose control if she didn't stop talking. She dropped her voice for the last bit. "*I* do care. I care about a helpless woman out there alone in the mountains. And I care about Papa. I *will* accomplish what he asked of us."

Rosie studied her, brows knit as though she didn't understand why Faith was so upset. She reached out and touched Faith's arm, and it took everything within her not to jerk away.

"*I* care, Faithie. We all do. It's just that we also have to take care of those still with us on this earth. Those who are expecting—" She waved a hand around. "Our family. The ranch. We have responsibilities. Papa would understand that responsibility better than anyone. He would want us to wait for the right time." Her face softened as her eyes turned distant. "I remember how he used to stay with the horses when they colicked, walking them for hours to help them recover from a twisted gut. He did whatever he had to."

Pain pressed in Faith's belly, a twisting that would steal her breath if she let it linger. She had no memory of Papa walking the horses when they colicked. It seemed all the good times had taken place when Faith was too young to remember. She was the baby of the family, so to her Papa had always seemed old—never young and vibrant—as far back as she could recall. The stories of his younger days sounded so thrilling.

Rosemary might be right about Papa understanding responsibility, but that only proved Faith's point all the more. They had a *responsibility* to find Steps Right and return those beads to her. The necklace had once been an heirloom within her own family, passed down through the generations.

Steps Right had been wearing the string when she discovered their father on the plains, nearly dead. While her sister had gone back to their village to get help, she'd stayed with Papa and nursed him through the night, keeping him alive and awake in the cold by having him tell stories of his wife and daughters. A story for every bead on the necklace.

She'd continued to care for him at her village, then when he recovered enough to rejoin his trapping companion, Steps Right had sent the strand of beads with him as a gift.

And as her papa lay dying, he'd tasked his four daughters—and her specifically, in that moment between the two of them—with returning the beads to her so they could be reunited with the Peigan family that had treasured them for generations.

Faith would fulfill that responsibility. Even if she had to do it alone.

Rosemary picked up the basket and turned with a smile. "We'll find her, Faith. I promise. As soon as we can." Then she started for the door. "I think Elise and Goes Ahead have arrived. I hear the children outside."

The family planned to set out tomorrow morning for a short trip to visit nearby villages they'd worked with in the past. Similar to the missionary journeys the apostle Paul had embarked on during Bible days.

How exciting it must be to travel so much. To see more of this vast, breathtaking land and meet its inhabitants. They'd probably seen a host of waterfalls throughout the mountains. They could have even been to the place where Steps Right lived right now.

An idea slipped into Faith's mind. What if she went with them tomorrow? They'd said this upcoming journey would be shorter than most, likely only a month, before they circled back to the trading post to restock supplies before a longer trip that would last through the winter.

She could accompany them. They planned to start northward, and White Horse had once mentioned a waterfall he knew in that direction. She could at least check that one. And they might even pass others she could search.

Hope rushed into her spirit, and she spun to gather Bertie and head outside. She would have to be convincing, but hopefully her sisters wouldn't mind her setting off with trusted friends to help share their faith.

It was time she took control of this search and accomplish what Papa had begged of them. Be the daughter he'd believed her to be. Then maybe the pain of losing him would finally start to heal.

TWO

Grant Allen eyed the horse preparing to race the flat stretch of land in front of him. Trappers and Natives had gathered in a line along the raceway, calling wagers up and down the row.

There weren't as many men now as there had been a couple weeks ago, during the busiest part of the rendezvous. But he still had to move his gaze slowly as he studied each fellow, taking in his profile. His height. The width of his shoulders.

If only Grant had a better idea of what his brother looked like now that Will had grown to manhood. He'd finally found the Sheldon family who'd taken Will in as a boy, after their parents died. But talking with Sam Sheldon hadn't helped as much as Grant had hoped.

He'd only said that Will was about the same height as Grant, maybe an inch or two shorter. Same color hair . . . nay, a bit lighter. Not quite as filled out, though now that Will had come west and lived a year in these mountains, he might be more so.

And now that Grant had spent a month in this western territory and seen the horde of trappers, he had a feeling there might be more changes to his brother's appearance. Did he wear an overgrown beard like nearly every other white man at the rendezvous? Or, at twenty years old, would Will be able to grow much more than scruff? Grant had shaved every day by that age, but more because his wife, Gloria, liked a smooth chin than any other reason.

"Hiya, Smiles."

The voice barely penetrated his thoughts, especially with that ridiculous nickname. Only when the young trapper nudged Grant's arm did he pull completely out of his ponderings to glance at the man.

Grant spared a nod, then turned back toward the raceway. This fellow had been one of the first in line to trade when Grant rode in with the supply wagons. Unfortunately, the young man's furs had been poor quality, so he'd not received as many supplies in return as he'd expected. Since then, they'd passed each other several times, and the man had somehow dubbed him with the absurd handle of *Smiles*, which made Grant want to *not* smile all the more.

The young trapper gestured toward the horses. "Already placed your bet?"

Grant shook his head. "Not much of a gambler."

"Suit yourself." The kid shrugged. "Got my eye on that buckskin." He paused. "Reckon he could help me earn the difference of what I didn't get on those sorry furs. What d'ya think?"

Grant eyed the animal. The dusky coloring with that black mane and tail was striking enough to catch any man's eye, but it was the *animal's* eyes that concerned him. The lack of excitement there. And you could just see the flash of white at the corners.

Growing up in St. Louis—the Gateway to the West—he'd had plenty of chances to sit on a street bench and listen to the old men talk about horseflesh. He'd once heard a gray-haired man say you could never trust a horse that showed the whites of his eyes.

Grant hadn't spent as much time around horses as a lot of fellows here, but he'd paid attention from that day on. More often than not, the man's words proved true.

Even so, he'd rather stay out of this youngster's business. The fellow had asked Grant's opinion, though. And if he bet on the buckskin against that leggy bay with the itch to move out, he'd lose even more of the supplies he needed to survive the winter.

Grant glanced sideways at him. He was about the age Will would be—twenty years. He couldn't actually *be* Will, though, not with that shock of blond hair.

But if Will were about to make such a poor decision, Grant would want someone to knock sense into him. He turned his focus forward again. "Save your trade goods."

The trapper spit a stream of tobacco juice onto a rock in front of him. "Nah, I need to win enough powder to fill my cartridges through the winter. You think the buckskin's the way to go?"

Grant shook his head. If the fellow was going to be bull-headed about it . . . "Saw the bay run yesterday. I'd put my money on him." Except he wouldn't. He knew far better than to waste his funds on a wager.

"Alrighty then." The man trotted off to place his bet, and Grant shifted his focus to those lining the far side of the raceway. He'd already questioned many of them, but none had heard of Will Sheldon. Nor Will Allen. He couldn't be sure whether his brother had used the surname of the family who took him in or kept their real name.

As he finished studying the figures on the far side, the horses moved into position for the riders to mount. It would be a few minutes before they shot the starting gun.

And there came that young trapper, trotting back toward him, a grin as wide as the Mississippi River spread across his face. They should call *him* Smiles.

Grant couldn't help a surge of sympathy. He'd been a boy once, desperate to make sure he'd have enough to eat, willing to take a chance. He'd thought his choices had paid off, once upon a time. He'd managed to secure a wife far above his position in St. Louis society. And he'd become son-in-law and assistant to one of the leading solicitors in the city.

He should have known it wouldn't last.

The trapper settled in beside him to watch the race. "Thanks for the tip. That bay is a real beauty."

Grant nodded. Was it too much to hope the fellow would catch on and learn to appreciate silence?

"I heard somethin' that might help *you*. A tip in return, you might say."

He spared the annoying man a look but still held his tongue. Just raised his brows and waited.

"Didn't you say your brother's name was Will . . . Shelton or somethin'?"

Grant's pulse quickened. "Sheldon."

The trapper nodded. "That's it. I was standin' at Parson's campfire, sharin' a cup of coffee and talkin' about the best places to trap this winter. I heared a couple fellows on

24

t'other side of the flame say the name *Will*. Got nosy, I did. An' when I asked about this Will fellow, they said it was a friend of their'n who was livin' in a cabin somewhere up on the Shaheela River. Said they thought they might find themselves there come the first snow an' see if they could bed down outta the weather."

Grant worked to keep his breathing even and not grab the man's shoulders to shake more details out of him. "Where's the Shaheela River? Who is Parson?" He'd not heard of a trapper by that name. Was that a surname or a profession? The men in these parts seemed to have a penchant for labeling each other with strange handles.

The boy turned and lifted an arm to point toward the lodges scattered around the valley. Before he could speak, a surge from the crowd lining the raceway spun him back toward the horses. "They're about to start."

With the blast of the gunshot, the voices around them surged almost as fast as the racing horses. Beside him, the trapper jumped and fisted the air, cheering on the bay with a colorful assortment of encouragements. "Come on, you mangy piece o' hide. Stretch those toothpicks. Move on past that dog-nosed blighter. Move on, I tell ya."

Grant didn't worry about tracking the animals down the raceway. His mind could only focus on what this overly friendly lad had revealed. The Shaheela River. It wasn't on the map he'd purchased before coming west, a sketch created from the details William Clark had drawn during the expedition he and Meriwether Lewis led to the Pacific Ocean.

As soon as the bay crossed the finish line two lengths in front of the buckskin, the young trapper started to run toward the crowd gathering around the winner. Grant grabbed his arm just in time and held him back. He couldn't let this first lead slip out of his hands.

The fellow tried to pull away. "I have to collect my winnings."

Grant gripped him harder. "Tell me where to find those men. The ones who know my brother."

The boy pointed again toward the lodges. "That bigger teepee with the square tent pitched beside it. Tell 'em Riggs sent you."

Finally, Grant could fulfill the promise he'd made all those years ago. He'd find Will. Make sure his brother was all right and help him in any way he could. Then he'd figure out what he intended to do with his own life.

Maybe he'd stay with Will and be a trapper in these Rocky Mountains. Two brothers, finally reunited after being torn apart so many years ago.

Maybe.

~

The roar of water crashing against massive rocks filled Faith's ears as she stepped closer to the waterfall. Mist rose from the cascading flow, creating a rainbow of colors in the pale morning light.

She squinted into the icy spray. Was there a cave behind? White Horse said some waterfalls in this area covered hidden tunnels, and he suspected his mother had taken refuge in one of them. Wouldn't it be wonderful if Faith located her on this very first search?

She couldn't tell if there was a cave here or not. She'd have to move closer to investigate, to see if there was a path leading behind. Steps Right wouldn't stay at a place where she had to drench herself—and maybe even be injured by the heavy flow—every time she came into or out of her home.

Faith moved to the edge of the falls where a path would be located. The mist sprayed a fine layer of wet over her face and hair, even her clothing—her favorite green cotton work dress. This was the only skirt that allowed her to move freely without tangling in her legs if she lengthened her stride. She'd taken to wearing trousers most days, but this had been one of Rosemary's requirements for her to accompany the missionary party. She had to wear a skirt at all times so the people they met would be able to distinguish her from the eldest boy in the family, fifteen-year-old Walking Bird.

Faith couldn't help if she was less filled out than her sisters. She'd always thought it was her youth that made her look more like a sapling than a woman, but at nineteen, she'd more than reached the age she should have grown more curves. It didn't matter to her if people confused her with a half-grown boy. But wearing a dress was a small price to pay for finally getting the chance to find Steps Right and fulfill her responsibility to Papa.

Her heart gave a skitter of anticipation. She was so close to finding the woman, she could feel it.

But there was no path leading behind this curtain of water, only slick, wet rocks.

Maybe the thick mist concealed a ledge, and a person had to simply step out in faith. She moved forward and crouched, feeling through the edge of the water's spray. Liquid pounded on her arm, drenching her sleeve.

Her hand met only a solid rock wall.

Maybe on the other side of the river? She stepped back to study the far bank, but her boot slipped on wet stone.

She stumbled, reaching out to catch herself. Her left foot slid out from under her and over the edge of the rock toward the river below, spreading her legs wide. She landed hard on the boulder, sitting spraddle-legged.

But too much of her weight was tipped toward the water, and the stone beneath her was slippery from so many years under the spray of the falls.

She slid sideways, crying out as she scrambled to grab something solid. Her hand caught a jutting rock just as she was about to tumble into the rushing water. Heart pounding, she clung to the stone with all her strength, both feet dangling over the edge.

THREE

Faith sucked in hard breaths, her heart racing as she struggled to get a foothold. Her boots only slipped off the wet rock. Should she let go and fall into the water below? It must be at least three body lengths down.

She couldn't give up so easily. What if she hit rocks in the pool? Or the waterfall sucked her under, raining down its powerful flow on her body? Could its strength break bones?

Gathering her strength, she used her arms to pull herself up and managed to get her chin above the rock. The edge of her vision caught motion on the bank, just in front of her. Then a hand gripped her arm. The thick fingers of a man.

Faith glanced up as she was lifted. The stranger grabbed her other arm and hauled her onto the rock, the stone scraping her belly through her wet clothing. The moment she reached solid ground, she turned her body to sit, taking in her rescuer.

A man, wearing the same kind of loose cotton shirt and trousers most of the trappers wore in the summer. Except he was clean-shaven, his hair not grown long like the men who traveled in this country. He wasn't too old either. Somewhere in his twenties.

That thought made her a little self-conscious as she still sat on the ground, her skirts twisted around her legs. "Thank you."

He nodded and stepped back, putting more distance between them. "Be more careful. You could have drowned."

She worked to keep from frowning. He didn't have to be rude about it. "I'm sorry to have bothered you." She worked for something close to a smile.

His brows gathered in a scowl. "It's your safety you should be concerned about. What are you doing out here?" He glanced around, and of course he didn't see anyone who might be her companion. His expression was a bit darker when he turned back to her. "Are you here alone?"

Perhaps she should be miffed by such an impertinent question. He didn't act as though he would take advantage of that fact, so he must be a decent sort. Despite his growling.

He might think it improper for a woman to explore a waterfall without companions, but his opinion didn't much matter. As she pushed up to her feet, he stepped forward like he would offer help. But then he moved back instead. Probably still concerned about the *no chaperone* bit.

She brushed the dirt and leaves from her skirts. "I'm looking for someone." Maybe she should ask if he'd seen Steps Right. If he came to this waterfall often, he might have spotted her.

They had to talk loudly over the waterfall, so she started down the hillside toward the path that had brought her here. He followed but didn't respond. When they were far enough away to have a normal conversation, she spun to face him.

He jerked to a halt, then backed a step, putting that distance between them again. His brows must stay permanently lowered in a scowl. He would be handsome if he smiled, but this must be his way to ward off would-be friends and admirers.

She offered a pleasant expression. "I'm looking for a friend. A Peigan woman named Steps Right. She's older, maybe around fifty years, with long white hair. Have you seen her around that waterfall by chance?"

His mouth pinched as he shook his head. "Yesterday was the first time I've been here."

He didn't ask why she was looking for a Native woman more than twice her age. Didn't ask why she would be searching so close to the falls. Didn't say anything else at all.

And just to spite him, or maybe make him uncomfortable, she should answer those questions he didn't care enough to ask. She wasn't normally given to talking overmuch, but something about this man made her want to step forward and poke his chest. Move into his space and push until she cracked the grumpy façade he wore like porcupine quills.

She squared her shoulders and smiled. "Steps Right is a woman my father met many years ago when he and a friend came to this land to trap through the winter. She saved his life, and now he's asked us to return a gift to her. We've located her son but are still looking for the woman herself. We have reason to believe she might be staying near a waterfall. This is the first one I've searched, and I thought maybe there would be a cave behind the water. That's why I got so close. But there's not a cave here. I guess I'll have to keep looking."

31

The longer she talked, the more his scowl relaxed. It had now faded completely into a raised-brow look that said he either didn't believe her story or couldn't fathom how he'd come to be standing in this mountain wilderness listening to a white woman prattle on so.

Either way made her want to grin more.

She propped her hands on her waist and tipped her head at him. "You don't know of any other waterfalls in the area, do you? Perhaps to the north or northeast?" Maybe there would be others along the route Elise and Goes Ahead planned to take.

His brows dipped again, and she almost regretted asking. But this expression was more thoughtful and less grumpy than before. "I don't remember seeing any that direction. Only farther west."

She straightened. "You've traveled a lot through these parts?" The rendezvous was happening somewhere around here, though Elise had said they wouldn't be venturing close to it. He must be a trapper who'd come to stock up on supplies.

But he shook his head. "I came with the supply wagons. I have a map that shows the terrain. Waterfalls too." He reached into the pocket sewn into his waistband and pulled out a paper folded into a small square.

He lifted a wary glance to her as he unfolded the document, as though he wasn't sure he should reveal this secret. It was all she could do not to jerk the paper from his hands and feast her eyes on its contents. But she dropped her hands to her sides as she leaned forward to see what he opened up.

Pencil marks covered the surface, and it took her a moment to make sense of lines and curves. He pointed to a tiny cloud on the left side. "This is where we are. That's the falls you almost died in."

She rolled her eyes, but he didn't look up to see her.

He pointed to an area near the middle of the page. "There's a waterfall here. Then two more along this river here. And another there." He slid his finger to the right side.

Excitement tingled through her. "Where are they? How far, and is there a trail?"

He hesitated before answering, as though weighing the risks of sharing the information with her. "They're all to the west. Not a place for a lady to travel alone."

"I'm not alone. I'm with friends."

He sent a glance toward the trail.

"They're back at camp." Maybe she was being foolhardy by making it so clear she was out here alone. She quickly added, "But I didn't come here by myself. I'm here with . . . my brother." The words slipped out of their own accord. It wasn't true, of course, but he didn't need to know that.

She glanced over the man's shoulder, then nodded that direction. "I see him coming now." She shifted her focus back to the map. "How would we get to these falls? Is there a trail or a road?"

The man looked where she'd motioned, then turned back to her. It was hard to tell if he believed her or not, but he was focusing on the map again, so hopefully she'd accomplished her purpose.

"I don't know if there's a trail. The map doesn't show it. You'd have to ask someone who's been out that way."

She lifted her gaze to him. "Do you know anyone who has?"

Something flickered across his expression, like a door closing. "I'm sure there are trappers who have. But that won't help a woman like you."

Urgh, this man was frustrating. But she held in her ire and gave an understanding nod. "My brother can speak with them. Do you know who he should ask? And where he might find them?"

Once more the man regarded her for a long moment. Too many heartbeats pounded in her chest as she waited, but she didn't back down. Just kept a pleasant—yet capable— look on her face.

"A man named Parson at the rendezvous. He's staying in a lodge with a lean-to tent staked next to it, near this end of the camp. I think he's been that way before, and he's getting ready to lead a group there again." He raised a staying hand. "You don't want to travel with those trappers. Just get directions from them."

Relief swarmed through her, and she tried not to let her grin spread too wide. "I'll be sure to tell him that. Thank you."

The man nodded, then turned toward the trail. He didn't say good-bye, but he certainly seemed to be leaving. Probably worried she'd ask more questions he didn't want to answer.

As he strode away, an impish thought slipped in, and she couldn't help herself as she called out to him. "Wait, I didn't catch your name."

He paused and glanced back, his expression guarded. "Allen. Grant Allen."

Now she couldn't help her grin. "Thank you, Mr. Allen. It was a pleasure to meet you."

Once more he nodded and turned away. This time she let him go.

She had much to figure out in order to keep going on this search for Steps Right. She couldn't disappoint or worry her family, but she also couldn't lose her first viable lead.

Was there a way she could possibly accomplish both?

FOUR

A re you sure you want to go alone?"
Faith held Elise's hands, the woman who had been so kind to her these past days. She met her gaze, though it was hard, knowing she was misleading these wonderful people. "I'll be fine. Really. I'm leaving early enough. I bet I can even make it home in one day." If she were going home. Which she wasn't.

Elise studied her face, not letting go of their joined hands. "I'm not sure your sisters will be pleased with me."

Faith gave a gentle squeeze. "They'll be fine. They know I'm stubborn. But they also know I'm capable. I've lived here in the Territory for three years now. I can ride a day or two by myself."

Elise nodded, though she still looked uncertain. "This land does make you strong." Then she pulled Faith in for a hug. "I'm sorry you didn't find Steps Right. We'll keep looking on our journey and send word if we find her."

For just a moment, Faith let herself breathe in the warm security of the embrace. How long had it been since she'd been truly held by a mother figure? Her sisters would slip an arm around her shoulders sometimes, but not a true hug that wrapped her fully. Made her feel loved and cared for.

The burn of tears stung her eyes. And when Elise pulled back, Faith blinked to keep from letting them show. "Thank you for everything. I've loved getting to know you and your family."

Elise smiled and reached for her husband, Goes Ahead, who stood back a few steps with Faith's gelding, Two Bit. The Gros Ventre man came to his wife's side. "We will pray your journey is safe and you find the grandmother you seek."

Faith tried to keep her smile bright and not allow the shyness that always tried to creep in around this man. Though he spoke clear English, he carried himself like the warrior he'd once been.

Elise and Goes Ahead's story was fascinating, how they met nearly seven years ago when Elise and her brother came to this land as missionaries. Goes Ahead had been mourning the death of his Salish wife while trying to travel through the mountains with his infant daughter and young son. Elise and her party had helped them, and by the end of the journey, Goes Ahead had come to faith, and the two of them had developed an affection that became the start of a beautiful marriage. All four of their children traveled with them now as they continued their missionary work, even fifteen-year-old Walking Bird and seven-year-old Pretty Shield, the pair who had brought them together in the beginning.

Faith nodded in response to Goes Ahead's words. "Thank you." Then she reached for her horse's reins. "I'd better get going."

Once she'd mounted, she glanced over to the campfire where Walking Bird knelt. The rest of the children still slept in the early light of dawn. The youth nodded to her. "Ride safe."

She returned the nod, then offered a final farewell to Elise and Goes Ahead. "I'll see you again soon."

At last, she nudged her mount's sides and started on the trail south, toward the Collins ranch. Surely she could find the exact location of the waterfalls on Mr. Allen's map, search them all, and get back to her sisters before these friends finished their route and came back through the trading post next month.

She rode southward until a hill separated her from view of the camp, then continued a bit farther until a cluster of trees also stood between them. She reined in Two Bit and slipped to the ground. "All right, boy. Now's the time to get ready for the rendezvous."

She'd worked through this setup in her mind all day yesterday. Then worried too much about it when she should have been sleeping.

Moving quickly, she pulled her trousers and work shirt out of her pack and slipped them on. For once, her stick-straight figure would be helpful. The shirt fit loosely enough that she didn't even have to wrap her chest to conceal the few curves she possessed. She tucked the pouch containing the blue crystal beads for Steps Right under the neckline. Maybe it was too risky to have brought them, but if she couldn't get Steps Right to come back to the ranch, at least she would be able to return this long-lost treasure to her.

She straightened and reached to pat her head. Her hair would be a bigger challenge. Should she cut it? Maybe leave a little length on her neck like a young man who'd spent a few months out here? She wouldn't be able to add even the start of a beard, though, so it'd be better to look fully trimmed. Like someone who'd come fresh from the east, ready to start exploring.

But she couldn't bring herself to cut her hair that short. Not for a single trip into the rendezvous camp to get better directions. She simply had to pass for a young man long enough to get the information she needed. And tucking her braid up into a hat should accomplish that.

After securing the wide-brimmed hat in place and pulling on her boots, she glanced down at herself once more. Too bad she didn't have a mirror to check the parts she couldn't see. Her clothes were dirty enough to pass for a man's.

Her hands, though . . . She dropped to her knees and rubbed mud from the dew-dampened ground over her exposed skin. Her hands, her neck, even her face. It should dry before she reached the rendezvous and might even help her look like she was growing a bit of scruff on her upper lip and chin.

Finally, she repacked her things and mounted Two Bit, then let out a breath as she gathered the reins. "Let's get this done."

From the details her family and the missionaries had said, she knew approximately where the rendezvous was being held this year. And Mr. Allen's pointing yesterday had confirmed the direction she'd thought. Hopefully she could reach that valley in a couple hours of steady riding.

It turned out to be nearer to three hours before the telltale signs of smoke rising above the crest of the hill gave her the first clue she was nearing her destination. Her heart quickened, and she urged Two Bit up the slope. At the top, she reined in where she could just see the valley but wouldn't be conspicuous to anyone looking up this way.

There weren't nearly as many lodges as the first rendez-vous she'd seen three years before, when she and her sisters first came west. There were gaps between the campsites here, though, which probably meant a number of trap-ping parties had already left. The festivities were winding down.

She inhaled a breath for courage, then released it. *Protect me, God. And help me get what I need here.*

She nudged Two Bit forward, then adjusted her posture in the saddle so she sat more like a man. As they descended the slope into the valley, she could make out trappers wan-dering through the camps. A few looked her way, but she didn't hold their interest long as they continued with what-ever they'd been doing.

A lodge and tent came into view that matched Mr. Al-len's description, so she steered her horse a bit to the left, toward that camp. Two men sat in front of the fire, but she was too far away to see their expressions enough to know if they were watching her.

She did her best to look nonchalant. She would need to deepen her voice. How should she begin? Should she ask for the man named Parson? Or simply say she'd heard they were setting out to a place where they'd see waterfalls?

Faith took a deep breath as she neared the edge of the camp, then reined in Two Bit and dismounted. She left the reins hanging so he would stay ground tied as she'd taught him, then ambled forward.

One of the men looked older, with graying hair and weathered skin above his full beard. The other possessed a youthful face and a scruffy beard that hadn't fully grown in. They both regarded her as she stopped a few feet from their campfire, but the younger man showed more open curiosity. Both seemed to be waiting for her to speak first.

She started to smile but caught herself and shifted her expression to something a little cocky, yet not unfriendly. "Howdy." She made her voice as deep as possible without sounding silly. "Is there a fellow named Parson here?"

The older man tipped his head a little. "Who's askin'?"

That must be him. "I heard he was headed west on a trail that might lead to a few waterfalls."

The lines across the man's brow deepened. "Might be."

Parson certainly wasn't a trusting man. Should she smile a little to show she was friendly? Men didn't reveal emotion as often, but the younger fellow beside Parson didn't seem to be trying to conceal his curiosity.

She tried for an affable, open look. "I'm hopin' to get some directions from him. Maybe find out the best trail to find those falls. I've a friend who said she'd be staying near one of 'em. Not sure which one, so I might need to check all the falls in that area."

Parson narrowed his gaze. "Your friend's a woman?"

She barely kept from cringing. Why had she revealed that? He probably thought she was a fellow trying to meet up with a sweetheart from one of the tribes. "She's an old grandmother from the Peigan tribe. A healer. She asked me to bring her something."

She couldn't breathe as she waited to see if that would satisfy his questions. The way he was eyeing her, he must be trying to decide if he believed her.

She didn't let herself shift under his scrutiny. She didn't

exactly meet his gaze full on, but she waited. Keeping herself quiet.

His expression gave no sign of his thoughts, but at last he spoke. "You can join on with me if you like. We're headed there in the mornin', me an' six others." He nodded to the younger man beside him. "Skeet here is one of 'em. We'll be trappin' all along those rivers where the falls are. I can show you a few that aren't on any map I've seen. If you have a mind to learn trappin', you can trade fer a few kits afore we leave. If not, you can come along as camp keeper. I expect every man to earn his share, but I don't nose into yer business neither."

She tried to keep the surprise from her expression. She hadn't expected an offer to join the group. Trap with them? She'd always wanted to try her hand at it. But she didn't have time to learn the trade now. Maybe later . . . but not with a group of strange men.

She gave a nod of thanks. "I appreciate that offer. Any other time, I'd say yes an' thank ye." That was an expression she'd heard the trappers use. "But I need to move faster this time. My friend needs what I'm bringing to her. Could you maybe draw me a map, or point me to a trail that will take me to the area?" If he would include more falls than she'd seen on Mr. Allen's map, all the better. Coming here had certainly been the right choice. Maybe even direction from God.

But he shook his head. "There's not a trail. And there's too much ground to cover to draw it out." He eyed her. "Besides, it's not a route a fellow should go on his own. 'Specially not one who's green to the area."

At least she'd been successful in her disguise. But the disappointment pressing in her chest didn't feel like success.

He pressed his hands to his knees and stood, releasing a little groan with the effort. "If you wanna see the falls, ride along with us. You can tend the fire and cook meals. Help with the horses. I've got enough supplies to feed you. Be here at sunrise."

He turned and ducked into the lodge, a clear signal he was done with the conversation.

The other fellow still sat by the fire, but as she met his gaze, he raised his brows. "You in?"

That was the question, wasn't it? She pinched her lips. "Maybe. Need to do some thinkin', I suppose."

Then she turned and headed back to Two Bit before he could ask anything more.

FIVE

G rant eyed the rest of the group as he fastened the
tether strap securing the pack mule to his horse.
Parson seemed like a decent fellow to ride with.
From his words, at least, he appeared to know the land well
but not be too overbearing. Since Grant had never trapped
before, he would be one of the camp keepers, but would
also be able to set a few traps and learn the trade from the
others. All six of the men here had spent at least one winter
trapping, including Riggs, the kid who'd told him about
Parson's group to begin with.

Grant had brought his own mount and gear, as well as all
the meat from a bull elk he'd found yesterday. The animal
had just been killed, as the warmth in its body and the blood
still running from the gunshot attested to, but the hunter
had abandoned it for some reason. He'd waited nearly an
hour to see if the person who shot it would come looking
for their kill, but no one came. The animal hadn't been
mangled by other prey, so Grant cut out all the good meat
he could to use as his contribution to this trapping party's

food supply. Far better the meat be used than the animal's life and so much food be wasted.

Parson seemed to be looking around a lot as he loaded his own pack mule. The men were all here and accounted for, as far as Grant could tell. Even now, though, their leader was staring out at the hill that lined one side of the rendez-vous camp.

Grant looked that direction too, and for a moment he saw nothing. Then a shift near the top of the hill caught his eye. A person cresting the ridge and riding down the slope. He didn't recognize the horse, but whoever it was rode by himself.

He glanced back at Parson. The man was still fastening straps but seemed to be studying the rider from the corner of his gaze.

By the time the newcomer reached them, several of the other men, including Riggs, had mounted and sat waiting. Grant checked his cinch once more, then placed his boot in the stirrup. His horse tried to lurch forward as he swung aboard, but he tightened the reins and settled in the saddle, then reached down to stroke the animal's shoulder as he watched Parson talk to the new fellow.

They seemed to know each other, and Parson motioned toward the group once. The boy—for he wasn't much older than a youth, likely not even as old as Riggs—nodded. Then moved his horse past Parson and reined to a stop.

Their leader turned to the rest of them. "This here is Frank. He'll be ridin' with us as camp keeper." The man glanced toward Grant. "Consider him your helper."

Grant nodded. He'd just been promoted. No longer the newcomer to this land. Frank looked his way, and the lad's eyes widened a little.

Grant studied the man—er, boy. Scrawny and dirty, but something about him seemed familiar. Had he come to trade while Grant was working at the supply wagons?

He couldn't pull up a memory near the wagons that included this fellow. In fact, he seemed younger than any man Grant had seen out here. He couldn't have come to this land by himself. Was he the son or little brother of one of the trappers?

He took in the face once more, studying the nuances. Small features. Those blue eyes were familiar.

Then realization settled over him. Those eyes looked like the woman he'd met at the waterfall, the one who'd nearly cracked her neck on the rocks. This must be the brother she spoke of.

Parson started his mount forward, calling for them to fall into line behind him. Grant guided his horse in with the others, moving closer to Frank. Maybe he would have a chance to ask more about him and his sister.

Not that he meant to poke his nose into their business. He had no desire to tangle himself in anyone else's affairs. He simply wanted to find Will, as he'd promised to do when they were separated all those years ago.

But in the meantime, he could ask a few questions. Find out the story with these two. Frank must be here because of Grant mentioning Parson's group to the boy's sister. What was she doing while her brother joined on with these trappers?

For the first hour or so, Grant watched the boy. He rode with a tense posture, as if he was uncomfortable being around the other men. What would Grant have done if he and Will were in the shoes of these siblings? He wouldn't have sent his younger brother out into the wilds with a group of unkempt mountain men. He would have gone himself. But of course this boy's older sister couldn't do that.

So . . . if Will had set out on a journey like this, mostly at the mercy of the men he traveled with, Grant would hope at least one of his companions would take him under his wing. Look after him and see that he stayed safe. Help him learn the ropes, so to speak.

He nudged his horse a little closer to Frank's. "How old are you, boy?"

Frank jerked his gaze to Grant, his eyes widening a little. He sure was a nervous sort. "Nineteen."

Grant couldn't help raising his brows. He would have staked money this lad wasn't a day over fifteen. He'd let it pass, though.

He moved his gaze forward so the lad didn't feel like he was being interrogated. "I think it might have been your sister I met a few days ago. Near a waterfall southeast of the rendezvous camp. She was looking for a friend, I think." He could feel Frank's gaze on him, but he kept his focus on the rocky path down the slope they were descending.

After a few heartbeats, Frank answered. "She said she met someone there. A fellow who showed her a map of more waterfalls."

He nodded. "I assume that's why you're riding with Parson. To find those waterfalls and look for your friend?" He slipped his gaze to Frank to catch his reaction.

The boy looked forward as he nodded. "I'd like to see that map again sometime, if you don't mind."

Grant frowned. *Again?* He must have meant *too.* Maybe he'd not been able to attend school. Grant himself had been lucky in that area. The Flagstones may not have wanted him for anything more than their daughter's companion, but at least they started him off with a decent education.

Grant shook his head, his thoughts returning to the matter at hand. "Sure. I'll show you the map when we get back to camp."

Frank nodded, his shoulders relaxing a bit.

As they rode, Grant studied the landscape around them. They'd been traveling up and down tree-littered slopes, occasionally crossing a narrow valley. It would be easy to get lost out here if you didn't pay attention.

Frank finally seemed to settle in for the ride, and at least he knew how to handle a horse. They paused a few times throughout the day to rest and water the animals, but Parson kept them moving steadily.

The men didn't talk much. It seemed most of them knew one another and had traveled together before. Riggs, Frank, and Grant appeared to be the only newcomers to the group.

As the sun began to dip low, Parson halted in a small valley with a stream running through it, a few trees lining each side of the water. As the man dismounted, he started barking orders. "Each man unloads his own animals tonight. Water 'em good, then hobble 'em in tall grass, close to the camp so wolves don't bother 'em. Grant and Frank, you're in charge of starting the fire and cookin' up grub. I like a hot meal at night, but be quick about it. We'll bed down early. Need to cover a lot o' ground tomorrow."

Grant slid to the ground. "Aye, sir."

He moved to Frank's horse, where the boy was digging in his saddle pack. "You know how to cook over an open flame? Or would you rather settle our animals?"

Grant could do either. He'd not had much experience cooking at all until he joined on with the supply wagons coming to the rendezvous, but he'd learned enough to make a stew over a campfire.

Frank shrugged. "Doesn't matter." Then he slid a glance at Grant, a look that seemed almost to judge his capabilities. "I'll cook. Make sure Two Bit stands in the water till he drinks. He's thirsty, but he might wait a minute or two." He held out the reins to Grant.

A bit of defensiveness rose up in his chest. He could cook as well as any kid. And he didn't need to be instructed on how to water a horse. But he simply took the reins and turned their mounts and his pack mule toward the water.

It would be a long journey with these men. He'd best work on keeping his mouth shut and doing his own work well. Once he found Will, he wouldn't be dependent on this group any longer.

Faith stirred the stew in the pot as the men worked around her to set up camp. They were currently debating if it would rain in the night, and whether they should set up cover above the campfire.

Two of the men—Skeet and Hooper—were convinced the sky would open up in a downpour while they slept, and they almost had Riggs swayed to their opinion. Parson and Willard waved the notion off, and the old-time trapper in the group hadn't chosen a side yet. The man hadn't said much actually, just sat back a little from the fire and sorted through one of his packs.

Grant had gone to gather more firewood, enough to

keep them through the night and heat the remaining stew in the morning. So far he hadn't realized she was actually the woman he met by the waterfall. She'd thought he recognized her at first. The panic nearly made her spin her horse and canter away.

But she'd held her ground, and finally realized he assumed she was the brother she'd mentioned at the waterfall. The lie sat like a bad piece of meat in her middle, churning her insides. But it was probably the best scenario she could be in right now.

Grant seemed to be trying to help her. She didn't want him to feel sorry for her, but if they could work together and keep the rest of the group satisfied with her efforts, she could keep from drawing undo notice.

Grant returned, his arms full of wood, just as she was ready to dish out the stew. She filled the bowls and handed them out, and finally the men stopped arguing as they ate.

She handed Grant his portion, and he nodded. "Thanks."

When she settled back with her own food, Parson spoke up. "Good stew."

A thin layer of pressure lifted off her chest with the words. She only nodded to him, though. As she'd studied the men today, it seemed they all did a lot of nodding instead of speaking.

The quiet didn't last long. When Parson finished downing his portion, he tossed the tin dish beside the fire. "Finish up, boys, then bed down. Pitch a tent if you're gonna, but I want quiet in half an hour."

She gulped her stew faster. She could take the used bowls to the creek and wash herself along with them. The mud she'd plastered on her skin itched, and she needed to clean off some of this sweat. She could dirty her face and hands again in the morning. She also needed to find a protected place to relieve herself. Maybe if she went to check the horses and mules.

Tomorrow would be easier. Now that she knew what was expected of her, and now that she'd made it through a full day without ruining her disguise, she could manage the rest of the trip.

And maybe in the next few days, they would reach the first waterfall and she could begin her search in earnest.

SIX

Grant woke as the first rays of light turned the eastern sky gray, but someone already knelt by the fire ring, stirring the coals to life. It must have been the dropping of a log that awakened him.

He'd planned to be the first one up, to get things going before Frank arose. The boy was probably tired after their first day out. Grant sure had been weary that first week after leaving St. Louis with the supply wagons. Riding all day in the saddle used muscles a man didn't know he possessed.

Even now, he could feel the effects of the few weeks' rest during the rendezvous. His back was stiff, and his thighs burned as he sat upright and pushed his blankets aside.

His motion must have startled Frank, for the boy twisted to face him. In the half-light, Grant couldn't make out his expression, but the eastern sky behind him outlined the youth's silhouette—revealing a form that wasn't as spindly as he'd thought yesterday.

Maybe that was a trick of the shadows. But it sure did look like Frank had *curves*. Curves in places boys didn't develop them.

The lad turned back to the fire without speaking, and Grant squeezed his eyes shut, then reopened them. He needed coffee. He must not be awake enough to see straight.

He slid his stockinged feet into boots, then stood and reached for the kettle. "I'll get water," he whispered.

As he returned with a full container, a few others were beginning to rise, including Parson. They'd be hungry, then their leader would likely push to saddle up and get on the trail.

While Grant added coffee grounds to the water, Frank continued to nurse the flame. He'd already placed the pot of remaining soup close enough to heat.

Neither of them spoke until Frank straightened. "Watch this soup, will ya? I'm going to the creek."

Grant nodded as the boy slipped out of camp. He didn't go to the water closest to them, though, but moved downstream a ways, disappearing into the brush beside the bank. As the coffee finished brewing and the soup warmed enough to eat, Grant handed out full plates and cups.

Frank still hadn't returned. He must be taking care of personal matters, but was there something more? Had he been hurt? Or maybe found something he needed help with, but was afraid to call out?

Grant took up his own cup of warm brew and stood, then ambled toward the water next to the camp. He might be able to see the boy downstream.

He dropped to his haunches by the flow, washing the food residue from his fingertips in the cold current. He could just see part of Frank's body near the bend in the creek. He looked to be washing his face maybe. That was good. The boy had looked a bit like a street urchin yesterday with all that dirt on him.

53

"Time to load up." Parson's call came from behind, and Grant stood, then turned back to the camp. He could load his and Frank's animals while the boy put away the cooking supplies.

When Grant led the saddled horses to camp so they could load the last of the packs, Frank stood and hoisted the satchel that contained the food and cooking pots. He seemed to work hard to lift it.

Grant reached to take the load. "Anything else need doing?"

Frank shook his head as he scanned the camp. "Just tie on our blankets."

The boy's face was still dirty. In fact, it looked like fresh mud. Grant couldn't help but stare as he tried to make sense of things. Had he seen wrong when he'd watched him splash water on his face?

Either Grant was losing his eyesight—or maybe his ability to think through what he was seeing—or something wasn't right with this boy.

He took the roll of bedding Frank handed him and tied it behind his saddle while the youth did the same with his own. The rest of the men had already mounted and were talking through how far they might travel that day. Parson wanted to reach the first possible trapping spot by midday tomorrow, early enough they could set a few traps and see if enough catch still lived there, or if they'd need to move on to a larger lake.

Grant mounted first, then watched from the corner of his eye as Frank swung up into the saddle. His movement was sure and quick, like he'd done the act a hundred times before. He turned the animal toward the others, and Grant did the same. Whatever else was off about the youngest member of their group, he knew how to handle a horse.

The rain the men had been arguing about finally started midmorning. Not a downpour, but enough to soak them. By the look of the thick gray clouds above, they'd stay wet for a few hours at least.

The trail Parson led them on was an animal path through a mountain pass, not overly steep or rocky. Frank rode in front of Grant, with Skeet behind him, mumbling about how he'd told everyone it would be a gully washer. Maybe they'd believe him next time.

By midday, the rain still fell, and Parson led them into a cluster of pines thick enough to provide shelter. "Let's eat a bite here and rest the horses."

The food pack was strapped onto Grant's pack mule, so he dismounted and worked to pull out the smoked meat and cornbread Parson had cooked up before they left the rendezvous. Frank came to his side and took the food Grant handed him.

Something about the younger man standing so close beside him brought a sensation of familiarity. As if they'd stood like this before.

He glanced sideways, but Frank's hat shielded most of his face, since he was shorter than Grant. He could see the man's shirt, though, and again that familiar feeling swept through him—along with an awareness of the way the wet cloth clung to his body.

Revealing definite curves.

His mind struggled to catch up with what he was seeing. To process what it all meant. Then a flash of memory slipped in. Him, standing next to the woman by the waterfall. Showing her the map he kept in his pocket. She'd been wet, drenched from the spray, her dress clinging to her frame. To her curves.

Exactly the way this shirt outlined the form of the person standing next to him.

Realization swept through, souring in his gut. This was no boy. *Not* the brother.

The woman herself.

She must have realized something in him had changed, for she looked up at him, tipping her hat to reveal her wide eyes. Drips of water had run down her cheeks and chin, clearing away the mud she'd plastered there and revealing smooth, tanned skin.

His gaze dropped to her hands, which held a pack of meat. Fingers too small to be a boy's. They weren't delicate and pale like his wife's had been. The nails were short and dirty, the skin darkened from hours in the sun. But definitely a woman's hands.

He took a step back as his mind processed what this meant on the journey. They couldn't allow a woman to travel with all these men. He jerked his gaze to her face again. She could possibly be the nineteen years she'd claimed. When Gloria was that age, he'd just begun courting her. She'd been fashionable and coy and—he found out later—determined to catch him, if only to frustrate her father by setting her sights beneath his plans for her.

This woman was completely opposite of Gloria. But she ignited his protective instincts in a way his wife never had. Gloria had never needed this kind of protection . . . at least he'd not thought so.

As pain twisted in his belly, a new determination rose

within him. He'd not protected his wife the way he should have. Not at the end. But maybe he could redeem himself now, at least in a small way.

She still stared at him, like a frightened deer. Probably waiting for his reaction. He could start with learning her name. He didn't even know Frank's last name—rather, the last name of the person he'd thought was Frank. But she might have made that up too, if he'd asked.

He kept his voice low. "Who are you?"

Her gaze turned wary. "Frank. Frank Collins."

Grant growled and shook his head. "I mean who are you *really*? I know you're the one I met at the waterfall. What's your name? And I don't want a lie this time."

She wilted. Nearly melted in front of him as her shoulders sank and her expression collapsed. Her neck flexed as she swallowed. How had he not noticed the thin column of her neck? Certainly no Adam's apple there.

She opened her mouth, and he had to lean in to hear her quiet words. "Faith Collins."

But then she straightened, squaring her shoulders and lifting her chin to meet his gaze. "You're not to tell the others."

He raised his brows. "You're in a fine position to make demands."

She blinked, then a corner of her mouth curved. Her face lit, even with only that tiny movement. Her eyes twinkled. "I suppose you have a point."

He tried to hold onto his frustration, but that grin had a way of clearing his mind. He shook his head to bring back his focus. "You can't travel with all these men."

Her smile dimmed a little but didn't fade completely. "That's why they need to think I'm a man."

He scowled. "A boy. Not a day over fifteen."

She wrinkled her nose, but still kept her grin. "Fifteen, then. Will you keep my secret?"

"Ya'll huntin' the game over there too?" Parson's voice broke through their conversation. "Just pull out the meat and pass it around."

Faith—Miss Collins—sent him a final pleading look, then turned and carried the pouch of jerky to the other men.

Grant's mind spun as he pulled out the cornbread and took it to Riggs. "Pass it around."

He moved back to his horse to eat his own fare and think. He couldn't let this woman continue to travel with them. She could be in danger if anyone else realized her disguise. At the very least, her reputation would be in tatters.

But could he send her back alone through this wilderness? Did she even have something to go back to?

He needed to talk to her, find out her situation and why she was desperate enough to find her friend that she would attempt a trick like this—if the story about finding an Indian woman near a waterfall was even true.

She didn't come near him again, though, not while they rested the horses. Maybe she thought avoiding him would keep him from outing her. It would do nothing of the kind. He would find out more about her, then he would make his decision.

When they were back in the saddle, the rain finally began to ease, and the group continued their journey in relative silence. Grant kept his horse a few paces behind Frank—or rather, Faith—as she rode with the other men in the front. He studied her profile as they rode, the line of her jaw, the curve of her cheekbone. She was a beautiful woman, even disguised as a boy. Clearly though, she was far tougher and more adventurous than the kind of women he knew in St. Louis. He couldn't even imagine what Gloria would do in a place like this, riding up the side of this mountain in the midst of a group of grizzled trappers.

They rode in the same order as before, with Skeet bringing up the rear. They'd been climbing the slope of a mountain at an angle, rounding the side of it, and as they began to descend the other side, Skeet moved his horse and packhorse around Grant, trotting up toward the front of the group. He slowed his animals to a walk beside Parson, and the two rode side by side for a few minutes. They must be talking, though their posture never revealed it.

Just ahead of him, Miss Collins glanced back at Grant, her eyes a little wide. Did she think Skeet had realized her secret too? Maybe she thought Grant told him.

Part of him felt a bit of triumph. When a person deceived people, they lived in fear of being found out. But Miss Collins must have a good reason for going to such lengths to find her friend.

As soon as they camped, he would find a way to talk to her, even if it took dragging her away from the others.

SEVEN

P arson must have read his mind, for the man halted them to set up camp earlier than the previous night. They were beside another stream, in a wider meadow than last night.

"We'll sleep here." Parson hadn't yet dismounted, but scanned the land around them, his gaze roaming up the slope of the mountain they'd just crossed on the left side of the valley.

Grant glanced that way too, but there was nothing they hadn't already seen. He dismounted and kept part of his gaze on Miss Collins, lest she try to slip away and evade his questions. She couldn't go far, though, not for long. Parson kept a firm handle on his group.

When they'd all dismounted, Parson began speaking to those nearest him—Skeet, Willard, and Riggs. Grant edged closer, but Parson was already motioning those three men to set off. Then he waved for the rest of them to approach him.

He spoke in a low voice. "There's someone watching us. Been following all day, I think. Water the horses, then tie 'em on the other side of the water to graze where they'll be outta the way. We'll camp over there too and set a watch." He motioned for them to carry out his order, even as his gaze shifted back to the mountain.

Grant's gut clenched even tighter than before. He'd been so busy worrying over Miss Collins, he'd not even thought about an outside threat. That must have been what Skeet rode up to speak to Parson about earlier. If Grant had kept his wits about him, he might have seen the shadow of a follower too.

He led his animals to the water behind the others, and while his horse and mule drank, he studied the cliffside once more. That mountain ran almost straight into the next, and he focused on the ridgeline, then let his gaze move down over the trees and boulders. No sign of movement.

Parson still watched from the edge of the trees, so Grant turned his focus to his work. They needed to set up camp and settle the animals, and he still needed to talk with Miss Collins. All while being far more aware of his surroundings than he'd been.

He would need to help with a watch in the night too.

He took charge of the animals again while Miss Collins started the fire. Now that he knew she was a woman, her preference to cook made more sense. She'd likely had experience preparing food over an open fire. After seeing to his and Miss Collins's horses and mule, he unloaded Parson's two animals so the man could stand watch behind one of the trees lining the bank.

The men kept quiet for the most part, tension spreading through the group as they worked to unsaddle and hobble the animals. Everyone brought in firewood this time, which meant he wouldn't have to spend extra time gathering it as he had last night.

Miss Collins looked to be preparing something in the pot that included dumplings, and he crouched in front of the fire, near enough that they could talk quietly. "Can I help?"

She shook her head. "It's almost done."

He kept his voice low and glanced toward the trees to make sure the others were still gathering wood or talking with Parson. "While it finishes, maybe you can tell me why you need to go to those waterfalls so badly you'd risk your reputation and virtue, and even your life, in such a way."

She frowned at him. "I told you, I'm looking for a friend. I have something important to give her."

He narrowed his eyes at her. "Something that will save her life? Because it would need to be that vital to take such a risk."

A woman wasn't always so logical, though. It hadn't taken him long after he and Gloria were married to realize she thought through things differently than he did. He'd not always been as willing to slow down and listen to her reasoning as he should have. Especially at the end. He should have taken her complaints seriously, but he'd thought her pains a passing ailment.

She raised her chin. "Not her life. But something incredibly valuable to her."

Before he could ask more, Riggs approached and dropped his load of sticks and logs. "That grub sure does smell good."

Miss Collins turned her focus back to the pot as she stirred, and when she spoke, her voice dipped into that deeper tone. "I think it's about ready."

Parson had Willard stand watch while they ate, and instead of the usual mealtime quiet, he used the opportunity to give orders for the night. "We need a guard posted at all times. We'll each take three hours." He looked to Grant. "You and the boy take the first shift. Wake Skeet at midnight. Then Hooper at three. When light dawns, we'll ride out."

Grant nearly grinned at Miss Collins. He would have three whole hours of quiet with her. He'd get all his questions answered.

"Who d'ya think it is out there? Blackfoot?" Riggs sounded almost eager for a threat.

Parson shook his head. "Don't know. Can't get a clear enough look at 'em. Just one person that I've seen, but he might be a scout."

Conversation died down after that, with everyone working quietly to finish setting up camp. Once he'd helped put away the food supplies, Grant took up his rifle, checked the horses once more, and then reported to Parson.

The man motioned across the creek. "There's a tree over there wide enough to hide one of you. Maybe both, if you're still." He eyed Grant. "I'm assigning you with the boy so you can teach him how to do a man's job. I know you're new to the area, but you seem to have a level head on your shoulders. You up for it?"

Grant nodded. "I am." The last thing he wanted was one of these others to take the *boy* under his wing and discover her secret.

Miss Collins joined them, and Grant motioned her toward the water they would need to cross. "I'll show you where we're to watch from."

When they reached the tree Parson had been watching

from, Grant pointed to the ground behind it. "You sit close to the trunk."

There weren't other trees wide enough to shield either of them, only a few saplings, so he positioned himself just behind her. He would be able to see the landscape better but might be visible to a watcher, depending on their location. Maybe the shadow of the branches would hide him.

He studied the land around them for a few minutes, his rifle across his lap at an angle where he could easily point and shoot, should the need arise.

At last, he was ready to begin his questions. He kept his voice to a whisper. "You didn't finish telling me what's so all-fired important you'd risk everything to find an Indian woman."

She turned sideways so she could see both him and the mountainside beyond the tree. She sent a glare he could just make out in the moonlight. "I'm not sure it's any of your business."

"If you expect me to continue this ruse that risks your life and virtue, I'll need more information. Then I'll decide if your reasons are significant enough."

"You can't simply do it because I ask?" She lifted wide eyes to him. Maybe that was supposed to be a pleading expression, but in the shadows, he could only see the whites of her eyes. She simply looked frightened.

He tried to gentle his tone, though it might not matter since they were whispering. "Miss Collins, I was once a solicitor. I've been trained not to take a case until I know the details and decide if I'm willing to defend the client against the charges." Well, he hadn't actually been the one defending. Not yet. He'd been promised that once he learned the trade from the bottom up, he'd be appointed one of the partners. And part of that education had been how to decide if a potential client was a good candidate for their services.

She didn't answer right away, but something changed in her demeanor. She must be deciding how much to tell. His chest tightened a little more. He wanted to know everything, and he'd keep pushing until he learned all.

But a pang of regret pricked. He wouldn't like someone forcing his hand, requiring *him* to spill all his secrets and intentions. Certainly this woman should be allowed the same courtesy. He simply needed to know enough to determine if he should send her back to the rendezvous—or maybe waste precious time taking her there himself—or keep her ruse and watch over her as they continued on with this group.

When she spoke, her voice was barely louder than a whisper, easier to understand, though still quiet. "I told you the woman I'm trying to find is Steps Right, one of the healers in the Peigan tribe."

He nodded.

"She knew my father more than twenty years ago when he came west for a season."

He nodded once more. She'd told him that before as well.

"When my father was dying, he asked us to find Steps Right and return a bead necklace to her, an heirloom that had been passed down through her family."

"We?" She probably meant she and her mysterious brother, but he couldn't assume that.

"My sisters and me. I'm the youngest of four."

He tipped his head. "Four sisters? Any brothers?"

"No."

He nearly snorted.

She was silent. Maybe he'd offended her, but in truth, *he* should be offended. Still, he gave a verbal nudge. "What next?"

She let out a sigh. "After we settled his affairs, my sisters and I decided we wanted to come west and give her the beads ourselves instead of having the solicitor send someone to deliver the gift. Papa had told us so many stories of his time here, and we wanted to see the place that had meant so much to him." She shrugged. "We traveled with the supply wagons three years ago. Arrived at the start of the rendezvous."

He raised his brows. "You and three other women came to the rendezvous of '37?" He'd heard the men talk about that year. The biggest gathering before it or since. But as suspicion slipped through him, he narrowed his gaze. "Did the four of you dress up as men?"

Her teeth flashed in a chuckle. "No, actually. We didn't realize the extent of what we were riding into. Thankfully, one of the trappers we met at first took pity on us and helped, both with our protection and our search. We never found Steps Right, but that trapper is now married to my sister Juniper."

Grant's mouth pinched. That didn't surprise him. Most men around here probably hadn't seen a white woman since they left Missouri. Which might have been years for some of them.

"We did find Steps Right's son, White Horse. He said his mother was cast out of their village because of a misunderstanding. He doesn't know where she is, but he believes she's safe—at least he did back then. We also found a herd

66

of horses that were descendants of a pair my father sent as a gift to Steps Right for saving his life. My sisters and I started a ranch with White Horse as our partner. It's been three years, though, and we still haven't found Steps Right like we promised my father."

He was beginning to understand the bigger picture, and it made his chest hurt. A promise to a loved one she hadn't yet been able to keep . . . Maybe the two of them had more in common than he'd suspected.

He had a few more questions, though. "If you haven't found her in three years, what makes you think you will now? And why waterfalls?"

Her voice rose a little. Not enough to put them at risk, but enough to show her emotion. "It's frustrating. We started off looking for her all the time, but then as we were establishing the ranch, we didn't have time. Then winter came, and one of my sisters was in the family way. We did find a clue in a cave where Steps Right had been, and White Horse is pretty sure she was telling him she would be staying near a waterfall. But before we could start searching for her, another of my sisters got married. And we had to build a cabin for Juniper and Riley. One thing after another. Now there are two more babes on the way, and Rosie says she doesn't know when we'll have time to look for Steps Right again. But White Horse saw two men from his old tribe at the trading post. Men who were known as soldiers among his people. I have a bad feeling about them. We *have* to find Steps Right before they do."

His throat tightened. He could understand her desperate need to fulfill the promise, even when it no longer seemed to matter to others. "And that's why you came by yourself?"

She nodded. "I wasn't alone at first. I left the ranch with family friends who were traveling near the falls where I found you. I didn't find Steps Right there, but then you told me about Parson. I thought I could just ask him to draw me a map, so I left my friends and dressed up like a man to look for him. He said he couldn't give me directions, but I could join on with him. He said he knew of several other falls that weren't on your map. It seemed like too good an opportunity to pass up. And my disguise worked. It still does."

He could mention that he'd seen through it already, but part of that might be because he had met her before without the disguise. The others didn't seem to pay her much notice. And with this new threat, their attention was even more distracted from her.

But that wouldn't last forever. "How do you intend to search the waterfalls once we get close to them? I doubt Parson will escort you himself. He'll be busy trapping."

She nodded. "He knows I'm here to see the falls, not trap. He said he'll give me directions once we get close."

She did seem to have most of the details sorted out. Except . . .

"And what will you do once you find this woman? *If* you find her, that is. She may have moved on already." Or she might not still be alive, but that seemed an unkind thing to say aloud.

"I hope to bring her back to our ranch. I suppose I'll sort through that once I meet her."

That part was *not* a solid plan. Maybe he could work out protection for them on the journey back. Perhaps he would have found Will by then, and his brother would be willing to go with him to accompany the two women safely to her sisters.

He studied her, as much as he could see in the darkness. If he refused to keep her secret and forced her to return to her sisters, he had a feeling Miss Faith Collins would find another way to leave and search for this elderly Peigan woman. And she might not stumble across someone who would ensure her safety like he would.

In fact, chances were good she *wouldn't* find a protector. He nearly snorted. He'd already proven ill-suited to protect a woman in his care. But if he was the only one here to do it, hopefully he could be better than no one.

He sighed. "All right. I'll keep your secret."

She let out a breath. "Thank you, Grant. Thank you so very much."

He couldn't help adding, "But if at any point I think my silence is putting you in danger, I'll speak up. I won't stand by and let harm come to you."

Her teeth flashed in the darkness. "I appreciate that."

EIGHT

The men were still on edge the next day, yet Faith could finally breathe again. Knowing that Grant not only knew her secret but also promised to help her keep it and protect her should she need a hand in that area, well . . . she'd never realized how wonderful it was to have a friend.

She usually had one or all of her sisters around during a new adventure. In fact, she couldn't ever remember going on an excursion without one of them.

Grant hadn't treated her differently today, though every now and then he gave her a long look that might garner notice from some of the others if they weren't so preoccupied with watching for whoever was following them. Grant had also stumbled when speaking her name once, nearly calling her Miss Collins. She needed to make it clear he should think of her even in his mind as Frank.

They'd finally reached the lake where Parson wanted to set traps this afternoon. Most of the men had already unloaded their possibles sacks and metal traps, and headed in different directions to claim an area they thought most likely to produce results.

She and Grant had been tasked with unpacking the animals and preparing the evening meal. Now they'd just about finished hobbling the horses and mules.

Grant straightened and patted the bay he'd just secured. "I'll get a fire started."

"I thought I'd make another stew tonight and start some beans soaking so we can cook them in the morning." That would be a nice change from meat stew every meal. After the dumplings last night, Parson had mentioned she should try to avoid using flour more than once a week. They'd only brought one small barrel of cornmeal too, which didn't leave much except beans and meat.

After tightening the knot in the hobble securing her last mule, she stood and stroked the animal's shoulder as she readjusted the pouch holding the necklace for Steps Right beneath her shirt. "Enjoy that grass. We'll be back to water you before nightfall."

She strode toward the camp, picking her way around the animals tearing at the rich grass that covered this valley. Grant had already gathered a pile of wood and now held the tinderbox, preparing to strike the flint and steel.

She moved to the food sack and reached down for it, but a flash of light jerked her gaze up.

Grant threw the tinderbox into the air just as a boom exploded in a puff of powder.

Shouts sounded from the others, and her heart surged into her throat. Was that a gunshot? Had Grant been hit?

He stood there, hands spread, staring at the tinderbox as it landed on the ground in shards.

"Are you hurt?" She moved to his side and touched his shoulder.

That contact seemed to push him into action. He stepped back, gripping her arm and pulling her with him. "Get away from it. I don't know what happened."

Parson came running, his breath heaving as he halted beside them. "What happened? Are you shot?"

Grant motioned toward the tinderbox, releasing her arm as he strode forward to pick it up. "Not shot. But this exploded when I lit a spark."

"Let me see it." Parson took the tinderbox from Grant's hand and examined the mangled case. His mouth pinched tight as he looked up at Grant. "There's residue from gunpowder in here."

She blinked. "How did that get there?"

Grant jerked his head to her with a frown. Only then did she realize she'd forgotten to deepen her voice. Parson didn't seem to notice, though.

The man looked around at the others who'd gathered. "Anyone know why there'd be gunpowder in the tinderbox?" He swung his gaze around them slowly, even eyeing her before turning to Grant himself.

"You think one of us put it there?" Grant raised his brows. "You think I'd blow my own hand off?"

Parson straightened. "I didn't say what I think. I simply asked a question."

Grant didn't back down. "It's my own personal tinderbox. I'd be the last one to tamper with it."

Parson frowned. "It looks like the one I brought for the camp keepers to use."

Grant shook his head. "It came from the supply wagons

like yours did, but this was a gift for my service on the journey out. You'll find my initials carved on the underside."

Parson flipped it over, his brows drawing lower before raising again. He looked up and turned to the others again. "I'll say it again. Does anyone know who put gunpowder in Grant's tinderbox?"

The knot in her middle pulled even tighter. Who would do such a thing? Was it a prank done by someone who thought it was the general lighter?

She couldn't help a glance at Riggs. He seemed the only one young and reckless enough to do such a thing, but even he would know a trick like that would be dangerous.

But the shock and horror in his expression couldn't be feigned, could it?

Willard was the first to speak, his voice a bit of a growl. "That's a serious thing you're accusin' us of." He glanced around at the others. "Any o' you boys put gunpowder in the man's tinderbox?"

The men responded with "No" and "'Course not."

Willard turned back to Parson. "We didn't do it. I 'spect you better look elsewhere for yer scoundrel." He sent a glare past Parson to Grant. "Maybe he's tryin' to get notice for hisself. Make the rest of us look bad."

She stiffened. Why would he think Grant would do such a dangerous thing to himself?

Grant's eyes narrowed. "I have no reason to put gunpowder in my own tinderbox. Nor do I want to blame anyone for it unjustly."

Parson raised a hand, his voice stern. "Enough. Maybe it's not one of us. Or maybe it was an accident." His gaze slipped back the way they'd come, probably searching for any sign of followers.

He turned back to the men and flapped his hand at them. "Go on an' finish setting traps. I doubt we'll stay here, but I wanna know if the trappin' is good first."

As the group dispersed, Grant turned to Faith. His dark eyes bored into her, and he kept his voice low. "Be careful. Take precautions in everything you do."

A shiver slid through her. "You think one of *them* was trying to hurt you?"

His jaw locked. "I'm more worried they were trying to hurt *you*. You're usually the one who starts the campfire. They might have thought that was the tinderbox you were going to use."

She wrapped her arms around herself, and her gaze slipped to where Riggs and Skeet knelt by a trap near the water. "I'll be careful."

She couldn't bring herself to ask the question that rose in her mind. Did they suspect her deception?

⁂

She had to get away.

The men had finished setting their traps, and all were lying around camp, mending or cleaning supplies. But mostly ogling Faith. Did they suspect her real identity? Or were they suspicious that she'd placed the gunpowder?

Grant saw it too, and was acting as protective as a mother bear, aiming curt remarks at any man who looked overlong in her direction. He didn't say anything to reveal her gender, just turned the man's attention elsewhere. But how long before he blundered?

She needed time away from all these men. Just a few minutes to walk along the creek and talk in a voice that wasn't so artificially deep it strained her throat.

As soon as she ladled the last bowl of stew and handed it to Grant, she stood. "I'm going to the creek." She sent him a look that he would hopefully interpret as *Don't come after me.*

He nodded, his eyes holding their own warning. "Be careful out there. It'll be full dark soon."

She kept her face neutral as she nodded and turned to walk away. The cooler air this evening brought a small relief as she walked, her steps quickening to put distance between herself and the camp. The sound of the creek rushing over rocks eased her spirit as she neared the water. She took a deep breath and let it out slowly, trying to ease the knot in her chest.

This little stream flowed into the lake where the men had set their traps. Its water was too shallow for there to be a waterfall farther upstream. And Parson knew she wanted to see every falls around the area they traveled, so he would have said something if he knew of one along this waterway.

But still, she followed the trickle up the slope. This wasn't a full mountain, just a boulder-strewn hill easy to maneuver in the half-light of evening. The effort stretched her limbs and cleared her mind. But as the incline became rockier and more vertical, the murmur of the water grew louder.

Could there be a waterfall here after all?

Shrubby brush clung to the sides of the creek, concealing the water unless she stood right next to it. One particular slope required her to move away from the stream to maneuver the climb upward. When she worked back to the edge of the bank, the louder rustling stirred hope in her chest.

She pushed aside the branches to reveal a pool at least a horse-length wide. A small fall of water spilled into it from a height as tall as her head.

A lovely setting, and possibly considered a waterfall, though nothing grand like the one where she'd met Grant.

Still, she should explore the area thoroughly. Steps Right could be here.

The rock behind the falling water clearly held no opening, so she climbed farther up the slope, then searched a distance away from the stream in both directions. With so many boulders, she had to take care to push aside the grass and brush around every one of them.

White Horse had showed them how easily a cave could be concealed by a small tree and a rock placed at just the right angle in front of the opening.

She found nothing, though. This must not be the right waterfall. She hadn't really thought it would be, but . . .

As she stood in the darkness next to the rustle of cascading water, she raised her voice loud enough that someone nearby would hear. "Steps Right, are you there? I'm a friend of your son, White Horse. You saved my father many years ago, and I've come to bring you a gift from him."

She wasn't certain how much English the woman understood, but probably not as much as she'd just spoken. Not that she was actually hiding nearby, listening. Still . . . "Steps Right. If you're there, speak to me. I come in peace."

Only the murmur of the water answered.

She released a long sigh. She should go back to camp now. Parson would have the men bedding down soon, so she wouldn't have to worry about evading questions or suspicious looks. If he was planning to post a watch as he'd done the past two nights, she would need to know her assigned time.

Pushing one foot forward, then the other, she started down the slope. At least this walk would be easier than the climb up.

She'd only gone halfway when the click of a rock skittering against another stone came from the line of trees ahead. She froze, straining to hear in the darkness.

"Faith?"

The sound of Grant's voice eased the weight on her chest, and she exhaled a long breath. She couldn't even be frustrated with him for following. She didn't have to keep a wary façade in place around him. She could be herself, and the thought of a friend to ease the disappointment beckoned.

So she called softly, "I'm here."

He stomped into view in the moonlight, a scowl shadowing his face as he paused to look at her. "Where have you been? Thought I'd find your dead body."

She couldn't help a smile. "Thank you for coming to find me before the wolves carried off my carcass."

He snorted and shook his head. He didn't appear willing to continue the banter as he surveyed the land around them, taking in the creek and the rocky slope. He nodded toward the hill behind her. "How far did you go?"

"Another ten minutes or so. I found a small waterfall and searched the area, just in case."

His expression softened. "No sign of your friend?"

She shook her head. "No caves. No evidence of people at all."

He gave a grim nod. "We'll keep looking. There will be plenty more waterfalls."

She started forward, and he fell into step beside her. They walked down the hill in quiet, but she kept her steps slow so they wouldn't reach camp too soon. She wasn't quite ready to face the others yet.

In truth, she'd like to know more about this man beside her. Despite his grumpiness, he seemed to be a man of character. A hard worker too, not given to complaining, no matter the lot laid on him.

How could she ask about him in a way that wouldn't seem impertinent? Maybe if she started casual conversation, she could lead into more interesting questions.

"What's happening back at camp?"

"A few of the men who traveled with Parson before were telling stories about the last time they camped here."

She nodded. "I'm sure their tales are interesting. Have you ever been this way before?"

"Nope."

That didn't work as well as she'd hoped. Maybe he needed to loosen up a bit first. She tried a different line of conversation. "Has Parson said whether we're keeping guard tonight?"

Grant looked toward camp before returning his focus to the shadowed path ahead. "Yeah. My watch is at midnight. You get the night off."

She shot him a look. "Parson gave me the night off? Or you don't want to babysit me?"

His brow gathered in a grimace that almost made her wish to take back the words. But she wanted to know the answer. And a direct question seemed to be the only way he'd offer information.

"Parson did."

She'd have to believe him, though a part of her still suspected chivalry on his part. Or maybe annoyance.

What else could she ask that would get him talking? She glanced toward the camp for inspiration. They would reach the light of the fire soon.

Her foot slipped on a rock, shooting forward so fast, she couldn't catch herself before crashing flat on her rear. Pain shot up her back, slowing her efforts to right herself.

NINE

Faith sucked in a breath against the pain as Grant reached out for her arm to stabilize her. She was already sitting on the rocky ground, though.

"Are you hurt?" He seemed uncertain whether he should pull her up or not.

Her bottom ached, but otherwise she wasn't injured. "I'm well. Just clumsy."

From the angle she'd fallen, and with pain radiating through her middle, she might need to turn on her hands and knees to rise. Not a ladylike position.

Maybe if she sat for a minute, she could recover enough not to make a fool of herself. She extracted her arm from his grip and motioned to the hillside next to her. "This is actually a nice place to sit. Won't you join me? The stars are already coming out."

She wasn't certain whether he would settle beside her, especially when he eyed the sky above, as if to see whether her claim was true.

He finally settled in beside her, an arm's length away, but

near enough it could be said they sat in companionable silence.

He stared upward, and she lifted her gaze to the sky too. A few dim stars twinkled above. The first of many more that would come on this cloudless night. The sky in this land was so vast, it filled with stars on summer nights.

Grant lifted his hand to point. "There's Vega. The buzzard star."

She looked upward, taking in the murky darkness, the few sparkles lighting the black canvas. He was pointing toward the center, where one star stood by itself.

"The buzzard star? Why do you call it that?"

He shrugged. "It's what the Greeks called it, back when they named the stars. Vega marks the beak of a buzzard carrying a harp in its mouth."

She couldn't help turning to stare at Grant. "A harp?" Who was this man who'd materialized beside her? Grant Allen did not speak of stars and Greek astronomists and harps. He rarely spoke at all.

His mouth curved as though he could read her thoughts, but his gaze stayed lifted to the sky. "The harp belongs to the god Orpheus. I think the Greeks called it a lyre. Orpheus could play such a pretty tune, it charmed the rocks and trees." A bit of humor slipped into his voice. "Unfortunately, he made a bunch of women angry, and they chased him, shooting arrows. In the ruckus, he dropped his harp. A buzzard swooped in, scooped it up in its beak, and flew into the sky with it."

He pointed to the star again. "And that's where they stand still today. The buzzard carrying the harp, suspended in the sky."

Silence settled again, but she couldn't help smiling at the tale. "That's quite a story. Do you know the secrets behind the other stars?" She pointed to another star closer to the eastern horizon. "Like that one."

"That's actually the planet Jupiter."

She raised her brows. "Oh." Then she slid a glance at him. "Does that mean you don't know its story?"

He chuckled. "I do. But it's a long one."

This side of Grant, the quiet knowledge, felt almost whimsical. And definitely intimate. It made her want more. To know the stories of his past, what made him take such an interest in the stars and Greek mythology that he'd learned them both so well.

She studied him. He felt her scrutiny, she had no doubt. But she wanted him to. Clearly, she had to be direct with this man to get answers. Besides, it felt good to finally show her interest. Just like when she'd been able to stop pretending to be a man around him.

He turned and met her gaze, his expression becoming a little sheepish. "My father used to read Greek mythology to us at bedtime."

"Us?" This was the first time he'd ever spoken of family. Or any of his life before the day she met him.

Sadness crept into the slant of his eyes, and he shifted back toward the heavens. "My brother and me. Will was probably too young to remember."

Was. Had their father died when they were boys? She kept her voice gentle. "You're the big brother, then."

He cut a sideways look at her. "And you're the baby of the family." He said it with just enough teasing to know he'd not meant it as a jab.

So she shrugged and infused a smile into her tone. "I guess that's why you're grumpy and I'm a ray of sunshine."

The comment earned a smile from him, and he refocused on the stars. Or maybe on his memories, for when he spoke again, his tone held nostalgia. "Will and I would catch fireflies in the evening, then lay out and look at the stars. I'd retell the stories our father read that included origins of the stars. For some reason, those fascinated me more than the rest." He turned a self-deprecating smile her way. "Or maybe those were the easiest to remember because the stars helped guide the retelling. A story for each star."

A pang pricked her chest. "I like that. It reminds me of the time my favorite horse died."

He sent her a frown. "That pleasant, huh?"

She chuckled. "The part I'm thinking of was nice. I suppose it didn't start out that way. I was out riding with my father at the far edge of our ranch, and Frances stepped in a gopher hole and broke her leg. Papa said there was nothing we could do for her. That the only kind act was to stop her suffering."

She pinched her mouth and did her best to pretend pain didn't still rise from the memory. "I couldn't watch, so I hid behind a big rock while he . . . took care of her. I wanted to bury her, but he said there was no way the two of us could do that. It was getting late, so we had to start for home or we'd be out after dark. On the ride back, I happened to ask what would happen to Frances when *she* was out after dark. Papa tended to state things bluntly, and he said wolves would probably come. I don't think he realized what my seven-year-old mind would do with that idea." She forced a smile, though his own expression turned sober as he listened, watching her.

She looked toward the sky again so she didn't have to face his gaze. "My nightmares woke Mama that night, and as soon as daylight came, she took me back to where Frances lay. Thankfully, the wolves hadn't found her. We carried rocks from a streambed that must have been a quarter mile away. Enough to cover sweet Frances. Mama and I told a memory for every rock we carried."

She glanced his way. "That's what made me think of it from your stars. A story for every rock."

He nodded, and the shadow at his throat bobbed. He was still looking at her, but his eyes were hard to read in the darkness. At last he said, "It's funny how the good memories get all tied up with the hard ones."

Her throat burned, and she nodded. "Yeah." The word scratched as it left her throat. That perfectly summed up that morning with Mama. "I brought back two extra stones that day, as keepsakes. One to remember Frances by. And one to remember how wonderful Mama was that day. She was always good, but what she did that day meant . . ." Her voice caught, interrupting the sentence. She swallowed to gather herself. "Anyway. Somehow the rocks got lost when Papa sold the farm and moved us to Richmond."

"I'm sorry." His words came quick and soft. But the next ones meant even more. "It's hard when something important gets taken away from you. Then lost."

She studied him. He spoke as though he'd experienced a similar loss. He didn't look like he would say more, so she asked. "What was taken from you?"

He sent another sideways look. "My brother. After our parents died, he was young enough that a family wanted him for their own. The day they took him away, I promised I'd find him. That I'd keep us together." He stared into the darkness ahead. "I didn't keep that promise for a lot of years, but that's why I'm out here now. Trying to find him."

She blinked, then glanced at the night around them. "Your brother's here?"

"Not in this exact spot." A smile played at the corner of his mouth. "But in this western territory somewhere. Skeet and Hooper said they met a man named Will Sheldon last winter who was staying in a cabin along the Shaheela River. That's why I'm traveling with this group. They're headed back to that place."

Pleasure washed through her. "You're going to be reunited. That's wonderful." She touched his arm to congratulate him. The contact seemed to surprise him, so she turned it into a light shake. "I'm so pleased for you both. How long has it been?"

His eyes glimmered with amusement as he watched her. "Fourteen years."

She pulled her hand from his arm. "I can't wait to meet him myself." And it was probably time the two of them returned to camp before she made an even greater spectacle of herself.

After pushing up to her feet, she dusted the dirt from her hands. "All right, then. Let's be off."

TEN

Grant studied the camp from his position at its edge as he stood watch later that night. He was supposed to be staring outward, searching for any sign of predators—human or otherwise. But he couldn't shake the pull Faith seemed to have on him. A draw strong enough that he'd told her about Will.

He'd only mentioned the stars on a whim—that alone should have warned him how close she was getting. But then she'd shared about her horse and her mother and the rocks. And she'd *lost* those rocks.

He knew how loss could eat at your soul. Chip away until you would do almost anything to repair the damage. She might never be able to find those exact stones, but he had a feeling that loss played into her determination to find this Indian woman.

They had this in common—the two of them. The ripping away of something special, and the desperate search to make it right again.

He let his gaze linger once more on the shadowed place where she slept, a little apart from the others. He didn't mind keeping watch. Not when it allowed him to ensure she stayed safe.

He turned back to scan the land around them—just as a powerful blow struck the side of his head.

Black swam through Grant's vision, but he struggled to keep himself upright. To fight back against whatever struck him.

Help. He needed to alert the others.

A shadow moved in front of him, and he lifted his hands to block another blow. Cold metal struck his face and arm, and he cried out as the force of it knocked him backward.

He grabbed at a tree to catch his balance and blinked to see through the haze of his mind and the dark of the night.

His cry had sounded the alarm, for shouts echoed from the camp. How many attackers would they have to ward off?

His gaze finally focused, but no one was in front of him. Not that he could make out.

He forced himself to turn, gripping tighter to the trunk as his vision spun. Trees lined the creek beside him, looking too much like people.

"What happened?" Parson said from just behind him, and Grant jumped at the sudden loudness.

"Someone attacked." His hand came up to where the first strike hit just behind his temple. That was the hardest, though his face stung from the second attack. "Hit me."

Parson shouted commands to the others, but Grant didn't worry about keeping up with the words. His head throbbed like a smithy struck a blow with every beat of his heart. He leaned against the tree and clutched his skull in both hands, trying to lessen the pounding.

"Where are you hurt?" Faith's voice sounded beside him,

far quieter and less painful than Parson's had been. Her hand rested on his shoulder. "Come back to the fire so I can see. Can you walk?"

He eased upright and took a step away from the tree. His head swam and his vision blurred, but he turned in the direction the camp should be. Her hand stayed on his shoulder, her fingers gentle and warm. He shouldn't let her see so much weakness, but in truth, he might not have made it to the fire without her guiding.

When they reached the center of camp, her hand pressed down on his shoulder. "Sit on this log."

He bent his legs and thankfully landed on the stump they'd used for a bench by the fire.

She crouched beside him, peeling his hands away from his head as she examined him. "You've got a gash on your cheek, and a knot already forming on your head here." She gently probed the place he'd been hit first, and it took everything in him not to wince away.

"How did this happen?" She moved so she was right in front of his face, waiting for his answer.

He barely caught himself before shaking his head. "I don't know. I looked at the camp for a second, then when I started to turn back toward the mountain, he hit me here." He pointed but didn't quite touch the spot.

She frowned. "Who was it?"

He pinched his mouth, trying to remember anything that would identify the attacker. "I don't know."

"Could you tell if it was an Indian?" Parson's voice sounded from the darkness, then the man stepped into the light to stand just behind Faith.

Grant could only give the same answer. "I don't know.

He got in two blows. I think they were both from a rifle, or something solid. I know the second was metal, though not sharp like a knife."

Faith brushed a finger down his cheek beside the place that stung. "That must be what caused this. The skin split, but it's more like a tear than a slice." She pushed to her feet. "I'll get the salve. If we take care of it, maybe you'll heal without a scar."

He nearly groaned. That's all he needed. A scar down his cheek to remind him and everyone he met about his time in the western territories.

Parson hammered a few more questions at him about where the attacker had gone and the person's size and hair color, none of which he could answer. When Faith returned to kneel in front of him, their leader turned back to speak with the others.

"Here's a cup of water. You can drink if you want, then I thought the cool tin might help if you hold it against that knot." She placed the mug in his hands, and their fingers brushed in the exchange. Her skin felt cool, which made him wish she would place her hand to his head instead of the cup. She would be much softer.

As she dabbed cream on his cheek, her face came close to his. He kept his gaze trained on the jar in her hands, but all his senses felt her nearness. His heart picked up speed at her touch, and her breath warmed his chin. Her fingers gently worked the salve into his skin, and he wanted nothing more than to lean in and kiss her.

But he couldn't.

When she finished applying the medicine, she looked up at him, her eyes pools of concern. "How are you feeling?"

He took a deep breath and let it out slowly, trying to calm his racing heart. "Better, thanks."

She nodded, her gaze lingering on his face for a moment longer before she stood and moved away.

He watched her go, his mind swirling with emotions he couldn't name. He couldn't let himself get so close to her again. This attraction that surged to life inside him had to be squelched before she realized how he felt.

He wasn't good enough for her, a fact that had been confirmed by every person he'd ever allowed close. He was through with letting himself love another. Except for Will. He owed it to his brother to find him.

But no one else.

Especially not a sprig of a woman he'd only just met, who was determined to carry out her own plans—regardless of what he said or did.

As Parson and most of the others drifted back into camp, he obeyed the order to bed down and sleep. Let another man stand guard.

He would keep his head down and follow orders. Not let his gaze be turned by a pretty face, especially one covered in mud and with a man's hat pulled low to shadow her features.

Then maybe both of them would get through this journey without fresh wounds added to the scars that already marked their pasts.

⊙~⊚

At least they were back on the trail today.

Faith squinted against the afternoon sun shining in her eyes. Though trapping at the little lake had been better than Parson expected, he chose to pack up and ride on the next morning anyway. Probably because of the attack on Grant. Grant had seemed better this morning, though the way he squinted probably meant his head still ached from the attacker's blow.

She'd heard some of the men murmuring about how the boot tracks they found were the kind only sold back east. That it must be a white man following them, not a scout from one of the tribes, as they'd assumed. But Parson hadn't made an official announcement with that information.

When she'd heard Grant ask him whether they found any sign of the man, Parson only said they searched halfway up the surrounding mountains and only found a few tracks. It must be a single person for them to attack the guard but run when the rest of the camp rose to give chase.

She scanned the trees that grew down the slope on her left. This trail wrapped around the side of the mountain, and anyone could lie in wait behind one of those trunks. The man hadn't shot at them yet, though it was likely he had a gun. Was he out of bullets or powder? Those could be hard to come by, though not as scarce right after the rendezvous.

Had he been trying to keep his attack quiet, then? That seemed more likely. He could pick off the group one at a time if they didn't all come charging at once. He might be able to do the same if he had a good hiding place where he could shoot them down one by one.

Her skin prickled, and she tried to peer into the shadows between the trees that lined the trail ahead. She rode just behind Grant, near the back of the line. Skeet followed behind her, probably because he was one of the more seasoned trappers, able to handle himself and make quick decisions should something happen up ahead.

With the long line of men in front of her, she should have nothing to worry about. No trouble from snipers hiding in the trees. Someone else would take the bullet first, though that thought didn't exactly relieve her.

"Halt!" The call came from Parson, then echoed down the line as men repeated it.

She fought the urge to wipe the sweat from her brow with her sleeve. It would only smear the mud she'd spread on that morning. Parson must think the horses needed a break from the heat. Maybe a small stream trickled down the mountainside. Some of these peaks still held pockets of packed snow, even now that August had nearly reached them, and the melt ran down in a steady rivulet.

The line shuffled forward slowly as the men and their animals spread down the slope to drink. They had, indeed, found a trickle of water to satisfy the thirsty horses and mules.

Behind her, Skeet split off into the trees down the slope at an angle. "This'll take forever if we stand here and wait."

His grumbling was right. Grant glanced at the man, then at her. He shrugged and turned his horse to follow Skeet's.

She nudged Two Bit after them. She didn't want to be the one at the tail end, holding the entire group up.

In the shade of the pines, the heat wasn't so fierce, though she had to brace against the lower limbs that slapped at her. One particular tree had several scraggly branches draping across her route. She ducked under it as Skeet and Grant had done.

A hand closed around her mouth, and another around her waist, pulling her sideways off her horse.

ELEVEN

S he tried to scream, but the hand sealed away any chance for sound to escape. She fought to free herself, trying to move her lips enough to bite down on the flesh covering her face. She had to alert—

"Do not fight, little sister."

The voice almost didn't register in her panic. Its tone and cadence were too familiar. Rote, like something she heard every day.

"Faith."

He spoke her name just as her mind was beginning to comprehend, her racing heart slowing enough to realize. But she couldn't piece together exactly what . . . She eased her fighting and craned to see the face of the one who held her.

White Horse?

She couldn't say his name with that foul-tasting paw over her mouth, but she could see just enough of his profile to know for certain.

The man she and all her sisters considered like a brother . . . was attacking her? Surely not.

He eased around in front of her, loosening his hold around her body. He didn't remove his hand from her mouth right away, but as soon as she could jerk her head back, she did so.

Then she scowled at him.

He motioned for her to be quiet.

She kept her voice to a whisper, but she didn't try to hide her ire. "What are you doing?" A new thought struck. Had Rosemary come too? She wouldn't have sent White Horse by himself to find Faith; she would have wanted to be part of the search.

Faith glanced around for her eldest sister. No sign of her, but Grant and Skeet had spotted Two Bit running free. They were already starting to call for her.

She spun back to White Horse. "Why are you here? You don't need to hide. I'll tell them you're my friend."

He shook his head. "Another looks to hurt them. They will not believe. I need talk to you. Tell them you need tree alone."

She shot him a look. "I'm not going back to the ranch, if that's what you've come to talk about. I'm looking for your mother." That should turn his thinking.

Grant had spotted her and was riding her way. She had to distract them. Or maybe she really should introduce White Horse as her friend. Would they believe he wasn't the one who'd been following them? The person who attacked Grant last night?

She spun and strode toward Grant. No reason to chance such a debacle. The last thing she wanted was to put White Horse in danger. Besides, he might not be willing to keep up her disguise as a man. She certainly didn't need that to ruin her search. She'd not had a chance to tell him about the ruse anyway.

She summoned a smile for Grant. "I didn't mean to worry you. I needed a moment to myself and tied Two Bit to a tree, but I guess he pulled loose." She glanced to the narrow stream where Skeet sat on his horse, holding her gelding's reins as both animals drank. "I'm glad you caught him."

She moved her focus back to Grant. "I'll just be another minute, then I'll be ready to keep riding." She waited for him to turn his horse and ride back to the others.

He didn't, so she stood there. Waiting. He must know what she meant.

Still, he eyed her. As though he suspected something more. His frown seemed stronger than he'd show from a lingering headache.

She shot a look at the rest of the group. "They're going to be ready to ride and looking for me. I need a minute."

His mouth pressed in a thin line, but he finally turned and nudged his mount back the way he'd come. Without saying a word.

The knot in her middle coiled tighter. But she didn't have the time to worry about Grant and whether he suspected something amiss. Or whether he was disappointed in her lying to him just now. Even as the thought squeezed in her chest, she pushed it away and moved back behind the tree that hid White Horse.

She scowled at him again. "Why are you here?" She didn't bother asking how he'd found her. White Horse had ways of knowing things that seemed impossible to know. Which was why it seemed so strange he hadn't located his mother yet.

That thought she pushed away as well. She could only hope he hadn't been trailing her all the way since the rendezvous.

A new suspicion slipped in. One she had to know the answer to. She braced her hands on her hips. "Did Rosie send you to follow me when I first left the ranch? Even when I was with Elise and Goes Ahead?"

A tiny grin touched his eyes, but he shook his head. "I trade two spotted horses at rendezvous. See you look like boy warrior. Follow."

Heat flamed up her neck, though she tried to stop it. To cover, she shook her head. "I'm not going back with you. This group is going to trap in an area that has a whole bunch of waterfalls. I think I'll find Steps Right there."

He stared at her. She met his gaze, letting her glare fall away, but also making sure he saw the depth of her determination.

He formed his own scowl. "Your sisters will not wish this."

She rolled her eyes. "Rosie, you mean. She still thinks I'm with the missionaries. I'll be back before she has a chance to worry."

Sadness touched his gaze, and maybe a bit of his own worry. His expressions were hard to read sometimes. "She concerns from her love."

She couldn't help a little smile at his wording. "I know. But I think she's forgotten about another love, that for our father. He pleaded with us to find your mother. To make certain she received the necklace back." She pressed a fist over her heart. "I have to do this for him. I can't let it rest the way my sisters have been able to."

Again, his brow lowered in what looked like a scowl. That stemmed from worry too.

She stepped forward and rested a hand on his arm. "I'll

be safe. Most of the men think I'm a boy. There's one, Grant, who knows who I am, and he's helping make sure I stay safe. Tell Rosie I'll be back around the same time I would have been before."

He looked down at her hand covering his loose cotton tunic. Then his gaze lifted to her eyes, and his own showed he was on the cusp of a decision. Had already made it but was calculating whether he should still change his mind.

At last he spoke, his gaze still hard on hers. "I go with you. Just we two. Leave these others. I know the water falling you speak of. We go to them, look for my mother. Then go to your sisters."

She caught her breath. That wasn't quite what she intended, but . . . would it be better? Traveling with White Horse would certainly be safer and more pleasant than being servant to these men. Except for Grant . . .

She couldn't let him figure into her decision, though. Maybe they'd meet again later.

Taking in a breath for courage, she nodded. "All right. I'll go with you." She hesitated. How would it be best to leave the group? Should she tell them about White Horse? Or just that she was heading out on her own?

"I'll go too."

The voice broke through her thoughts, and she spun to find its source.

Grant stood behind her, his expression a determined mask as he stepped forward. His gaze flicked between her and White Horse, and her insides clenched tighter.

She motioned toward her old friend. "This is White Horse, the one I told you about who's a partner with my sisters and me on the ranch. His mother is the one I'm looking for."

Grant gave a single nod as his gaze met White Horse's. "Hello."

White Horse only made a sound, and she dared a glance his way. He didn't show much of his thoughts in his expression, but she could make out distrust.

She tried to redirect his attention. "This is Grant Allen. He's been a good friend, helping me and making sure I'm not in danger."

White Horse's mouth only pinched tighter. He would need to see Grant's kindness before he was convinced. Better to address Grant's comments now.

She turned to him. "You're looking for your brother, though. Shouldn't you stay with this group so they can take you to him?"

Again, Grant flicked his focus to White Horse before honing on her. His voice softened a little when he spoke. "I've questioned them enough that I think I can find Will with the directions they've given. I actually think he could be near the cluster of waterfalls on my map. At least, along that same river." The lines at the corners of his eyes tightened. "I'd much rather travel with you than them. For one, we'll be moving faster. I'll reach Will sooner. And maybe I can help find Steps Right."

His words drew a longing inside her. This way she wouldn't have to say good-bye. Not yet, anyway.

She glanced back at White Horse. He still didn't look happy about a stranger tagging along. Would he refuse to allow it? Even if she pleaded? Surely she wouldn't have to resort to that. Surely these two men could simply get along.

She squared her shoulders and nodded to White Horse. "Grant is right. I trust him, and if we're both going to the

same area, it makes sense we travel together." She put all
the pleading she could in her gaze, willing White Horse to
understand.

At first, he barely looked at her. But when he did glance
her way, he must have seen her silent begging. He blinked
once, something he rarely did in conversation. It was almost as though he was trying to shake off the effects of her
efforts to persuade.

She pressed harder, adding words. "He'll be a benefit to
us. I'd like to have him along."

White Horse met her gaze once more, and his begrudg-
ing showed clearly in his slow nod. Then he turned his
focus on Grant, his eyes as imposing as a stormy sky. "You
ride with us." Unspoken was a warning she didn't want to
unpack.

Relief eased through her, and she exhaled a shaky breath.
"Good." Turning, she leaned around the tree to see the rest
of the group. "Do you think Parson will be angry at our
leaving?"

"Maybe. I'll do the talking."

She looked at Grant, but he'd already started toward the
others. So she turned back to White Horse. "Stay here. We'll
come back to you."

She needn't have bothered. White Horse would move
around as he saw fit. But it felt good to say something, as if
she had some modicum of control over this situation.

She didn't. But pretending so helped the jumble of her
nerves.

Was she making a mistake setting off with these two men?
Men she cared about, though in different ways.

Men who'd already started off at odds with each other.

"Well, I must say it's a relief to finally be a female again."

Though his head still throbbed from being conked last night, Grant eyed Faith, who rode ahead of him, beside the brave. She'd always been a female, but he certainly didn't need her to flaunt that fact. He'd had enough trouble keeping his thoughts reined in when she was plastering mud on her face and dressed in men's garb. If she allowed her womanly features more visibility, well . . .

Beside her, White Horse sent her a look but didn't say anything. The man was a quiet sort, but he spoke English well enough that his quiet seemed more from preference than difficulty with the language.

Faith had spoken of him as a partner with their ranch, that he'd become such a good friend she and her sisters thought of him like a brother. Grant hadn't expected that to be as true as it now appeared to be.

She rolled her eyes at the man when she was flustered, used a pleading gaze that no man—brother or otherwise—could deny, and seemed so comfortable in his presence that she'd looked relieved to set off with him *alone* into the mountain wilderness. To a place where only *he* knew the route. He could intend any sort of harm and she would be an easy victim.

Grant hadn't been able to let her go alone with the stranger. Even if White Horse really was as good a man as Faith thought him, *he* likely didn't think of *her* as a sister. What man could spend so much time around Faith Collins and not appreciate her spirit and determination? Where Faith was concerned, a single admiring thought quickly slid into an attraction that consumed far too much of his time.

Even if he could have no future with her—which he couldn't, he had to keep reminding himself of that—he could at least help protect her virtue on this journey.

Appearances and reputations might mean next to nothing in this wild mountain country but being violated—or worse—would be devastating for her. He couldn't let that happen.

He wouldn't.

Parson hadn't been pleased to lose his two camp keepers, but Grant did his best not to burn a bridge with the man, thanking him for allowing them to travel along this far. He'd left the pack mule with Parson, since both the animal and most of the supplies it carried belonged to the group.

As their trail climbed higher up the slope, the rocky ground turned more jagged. The sky was beginning to darken too, turning a steel gray that cast a pall over the air around them.

White Horse saw it too, for his gaze kept lifting upward. Finally, he spoke. "The rains come before dark. We make camp." He shifted his mount off the trail, down the slope at an angle toward a cluster of tall pines growing on the mountainside. Hopefully they could also find water in the area.

As they dismounted, the wind picked up, rattling through the trees and tugging at his coat. They worked quickly to unfasten the packs they'd need, then White Horse took the animals. "I take to grass."

There seemed such a small amount on this rocky slope, he'd have to move them frequently. But White Horse would find the heartiest section, no doubt.

Grant turned to Faith, who already knelt beside the food pack. "I'll gather firewood. Then we can set up a cover before the rain starts."

When he returned with enough branches to see them through a meal, Faith had already lit a small flame using the dry tinder they carried with them. She sent him a smile as he laid the logs near her.

A crack of thunder covered her words, and the lingering distant rumble made his pulse pick up. He needed to tie up an oilcloth posthaste.

White Horse returned as he was unfolding the cover, and the two of them worked in silence, tying the ends to trees. The man seemed competent and easy in his movements. He didn't send any glares toward Grant, just focused on working together to set up camp.

By the time they had things settled, the first drops of rain began to fall, and soon the sky opened up in a steady downpour. Faith had put together a simple meal of dried meat and johnnycakes, and they huddled close to the fire as they ate.

Even though they had the oilcloth above and the pine branches over that, the ground beneath them quickly became mud from water running down the slope.

They would all be soaked before this night was through.

TWELVE

Grant glanced at Faith across the campfire, and she met his look. The pounding of the rain made it too hard for small talk. But the smile in her eyes said she didn't mind the hardship of the weather. Maybe she was accustomed to traveling like this. Or perhaps she was simply relieved to be away from the trappers and back with an old friend whom she felt comfortable with.

He slid his focus to White Horse. The man kept his gaze roaming the trees around their camp as he ate. Not in a fierce way, almost absentmindedly as he chewed. But he missed nothing, Grant had no doubt of that.

Faith raised her voice over the rain as she turned to the brave. "How long do you think it will take us to reach the waterfalls?"

White Horse paused in his chewing, considering her words. "If rain stops, might be two sleeps."

Faith nodded, her gaze flicking to the rain outside their cover.

Two days wouldn't be bad. It was far less than if they'd stayed with Parson's group. White Horse would probably move faster, and Parson had spoken of stopping again tomorrow to put out traps and test how many fur-bearers lived in the area.

Grant swallowed his bite and looked to White Horse. "You said you know of the Shaheela River? Do you know how far it is from here?"

His brows gathered and his gaze turned distant. "Maybe one more sleep beyond."

And then likely longer to find Will once they reached the river.

But he was closer to his brother than ever before on this journey. He might even find Will within the week.

That thought sparked a hope inside him that not even bedding down on the wet ground could smother.

～⁊⁊～

Grant jerked awake, then froze in the darkness, his senses straining. The rain had stopped, leaving the air around them still. Too quiet.

Something wasn't right. He'd not awakened with this sense of foreboding in a while.

His eyes had mostly adjusted to the starless night, and he could see the shadows of trunks all around their camp. A threat could be hiding behind any one of them.

Why had they selected this cluster of trees to sleep in? The trunks allowed cover for an intruder to approach so close he could strike them all in their sleep.

A few raindrops pinged on the oilcloth stretched over them. Moisture that had gathered on the pine needles above during the storm, no doubt.

He moved his gaze around the camp. A few coals still

glowed from the fire, barely bright enough to show the rise and fall of Faith's shoulder as she slept. White Horse too appeared to be resting peacefully. Wouldn't his honed instincts have alerted him if there truly was danger?

Grant eased out a breath. Maybe he'd dreamed something that brought on this panic. He couldn't recall a dream, but that didn't mean he'd not experienced one.

He scanned the saddles and supplies they'd covered with a fur to protect them from the rain. In the shadows, something didn't look right with the stack. Was there a pack piled on top?

His heart picked up speed again as he slipped from his blanket and stood. He tucked his pistol into his waistband, just in case. When he crept closer, it was easier to see the jumble of fur heaped at the outside edge, as though someone had moved it aside to retrieve something from a pack and not pulled the covering back in place.

White Horse rose as Grant shifted around to the spot. He paused first to peer into the trees for signs of an intruder. No movement or unusual sounds.

The brave crouched down by the supplies. "Open."

Grant turned to him. "Which one?" But he could already see White Horse looking into the satchel where they kept the food. "Is anything missing?"

As he knelt beside White Horse, the man held the open bag toward him. Grant had been the one to pack these supplies away last night. He riffled through the contents on top. "Where's the flour? And the buffalo meat?" They were the last containers he'd put away.

White Horse stood, then moved outside the camp and peered at the ground. There should be tracks in the muddy ground, though they might be hard to spot with trees casting shadows on the ground.

A twig snapped behind him, and Grant whirled, his hand reaching for the gun at his waist.

It was only Faith, sitting up in her blankets.

He eased out a breath, releasing his hand from the pistol. He might have shot her if he was faster with his draw. Her sleepy look tugged at him, tightening his chest.

She rubbed an eye with one hand, the other going up to adjust the leather tie around her neck. He'd seen her do that a few times on this journey. She looked from him to White Horse. "What's going on?"

His belly tightened even more. She was so special, so delicate despite her strength and courage. He had to do a better job protecting her. Not allow something or someone to steal their food right under his nose.

He swallowed. "Some of our food is missing." He turned back to White Horse. "Find anything?"

The brave shook his head. "No tracks. Maybe see when light comes."

He frowned. "You don't know if it's animal or man?"

White Horse straightened and stared into the darkness beyond them. Then he turned and moved back to the packs, crouching to examine them. "No mark of claw. No bite."

Faith had woken fully, her eyes rounding. "You think it was a person?"

Grant scrambled for any other possibility. "Could it have been a coon? Are there other animals that use their paws like hands around here?" He'd seen more than one such creature in St. Louis extract food under the cover of darkness without leaving a sign.

For a long moment, White Horse frowned at the ground in front of the pack. Then he lifted his focus to Faith, though he was quiet for another moment. Something shifted in his eyes, a faint softening. He stood. "I will watch until light."

Grant glanced at the eastern horizon, though trees concealed the sky. He couldn't tell for sure, but the night probably had only another hour or two until dawn.

He nodded and turned back toward his bedding. He might not sleep, but hopefully him lying down would encourage Faith to do the same.

In the morning, they could determine exactly what had stolen their food. And if it *was* a man, he and White Horse wouldn't rest until they found the scoundrel. They couldn't let this threat come any closer to Faith than it already had.

From her saddle, Faith gazed out over the lush valley, her eyes tracing the path of the stream that meandered like a ribbon through the sea of grass. The rich blue of the sky stretched so vast and open it made her heart ache with longing. Grant sat on her left and White Horse on her right, all three of them pausing on this mountain pass to take in the view.

She eased out a breath as the beauty seeped into her soul, loosening the tension that had coiled within her all day. They'd found no sign of tracks around their campsite that morning, except for their own prints. No sign of what had stolen their food. Maybe it had been only a raccoon, like Grant said, creeping away silently with the food grasped in its tiny paws. Believing that eased the worry knotted inside her.

This view soothed her even more.

"Beautiful, isn't it?" Grant's voice rumbled beside her.

She smiled. "It reminds me of the valley where our ranch is." How were her sisters faring in her absence? Juniper and Lorelei were both in the family way. Was Lorelei sick with the stomach illness like June? And was June faring better this time than she had when she carried little Bertie?

And oh, precious Bertie. A fresh yearning surged within her to curl her sweet niece in her arms, squeezing her pudgy rolls and breathing in her little-girl scent.

"Creator Father gives many good things." White Horse's voice broke into her thoughts.

Before she could glance at him, something like a snort sounded from Grant. She raised her brows at him, but he kept his focus ahead.

White Horse must have heard it too, for he said, "You do not believe Creator Father gives all this from love?" He motioned toward the bounty before them.

She looked back to Grant to catch his expression. His eyes had narrowed a little, sealing away his thoughts so she couldn't read them.

He gave a small shrug. "I wouldn't know."

That seemed to be all he would say, and it certainly left questions swirling in her mind. Had he not been taught about God? Or did he choose not to believe? Or maybe he was angry at the Almighty for some pain in his past.

Her own chest ached with that thought. She didn't let herself think much about God. Contemplating His actions only raised painful queries about His actions in her own life. Why had He allowed her mother to fade away so quickly? That had been the starting point of every painful change in the past six years. If God simply would have healed her, Papa never would have sold the ranch and moved them to Richmond. Then he wouldn't have been out on the street that awful night when he was struck by the carriage. He would still be alive. They would all be together still, living that wonderful life on the ranch.

White Horse once more broke through her thoughts, but this time it was a relief. He signaled for Grant to lead them down the pass and into the valley, and she guided Two Bit behind his horse so White Horse could bring up the rear as he had most of the day.

As they maneuvered down the rocky incline, Grant's strong profile drew her focus far too often. In truth, he was a welcome distraction. His broad shoulders held an air of quiet confidence, his hands guiding his mount with a gentleness that seemed one with the horse. His kindness showed in the way he stroked the gelding's neck when it stumbled over a rock.

Grant had extended that same quiet thoughtfulness to her more times than she could count along this journey. His growling was merely a front for the noble man beneath.

God, why must you place such temptation before me? She could do nothing to make him show interest in her, not unless he truly felt such attraction.

There were moments it seemed he felt this same pull between them. Like the night he'd shown her the stars. But so many other times he kept himself aloof. Last night, for example, when they were making camp in the rain. He'd barely spoken, as though they were little more than acquaintances. Was she wishing for something that simply wasn't there? Misinterpreting his acts of kindness?

"Faith?" Grant called out, turning to look at her with worry in his expression, as if sensing her internal struggle. "Is everything all right?"

"Yes." She nudged Two Bit faster down the last of the slope, heat rushing to her cheeks. She'd slowed him too much, creating distance between her and Grant. A subconscious way of protecting her heart?

"Good." He waited for her and White Horse to catch up with him, and his eyes softened for a brief moment before returning to the path ahead.

After allowing the horses to drink in the stream, they followed its route for about an hour. At the end of that valley, the once-gentle creek grew more turbulent as it fed into a wide river. A high cliff bank rose up along the water's edge on both sides, creating a canyon the current flowed swiftly through.

They all reined in near the edge, and White Horse dismounted. Faith glanced at Grant, who met her gaze with a shrug. They did what White Horse, their dauntless leader, did.

The horses dropped their heads to graze, and she moved to stand beside her old friend, with Grant coming up on her other side.

"Is this the Shaheela?" Grant's voice rose above the rushing water.

White Horse nodded, then pointed downstream. "We ride until sun sleep, then reach first falls when sun two fingers high."

In the morning, then. A thrill slipped through her. They might find Steps Right before noon tomorrow.

But . . . she might not be at the first waterfall they came to.

Faith had to prepare herself for a long search. She glanced at White Horse. "Are there other falls close to that one?"

The edges of her friend's eyes crinkled just enough to know he was laughing at her impatience. "I do not remember the distance. We know when see."

She nudged his arm and grinned. "You remember everything. You expect me to believe you don't remember how far apart the falls are?"

Before he could answer, a shout came from her other side.

She spun, just as Grant jumped over the edge of the cliff. His arms flailed as he sailed through the air.

"Grant!" Faith screamed, her heart surging to her throat. Panic coursed through her veins as he struck the water, then his body disappeared into the churning current below.

What should she do? She turned to White Horse, but he was already climbing over the edge.

"No!" She dropped to her knees to grab him, but White Horse lowered himself before she could grab him.

He swung from one handhold down to the next, within seconds reaching the thin path that ran along the water's edge. He turned to scan the water, and she shifted her focus there too. Had Grant been carried downriver? Had he hit a rock and drowned?

God, no!

As she searched the water, a head finally bobbed in the current.

Grant.

He was a little downstream from them, but not as much as she'd feared. Was he conscious? She couldn't tell for certain.

White Horse had already run down the narrow path beside the water, and now he leaped into the flow. His

111

body disappeared beneath the surface for a moment before emerging, arms churning through the current in quick strokes.

God, protect them both. She could do nothing to help. Nothing except watch and pray.

White Horse swam toward Grant, using the current to his advantage. He finally reached him, and the two floated in the water for a moment. Talking, maybe? Grant shifted to fully look at the other man—the first sign to confirm he was alert.

White Horse grasped his arm and turned, then started swimming back toward the shore.

She had to get down to them. She needed to be there to help when Grant came out of the water. How much liquid had he swallowed?

She moved to her hands and knees and peered over the edge of the cliff, then scanned both directions for a place she could climb down.

There. She sprang to her feet and sprinted downstream to a narrow path the animals had made to the water. She slid her way down the steep trail and reached the bottom just as White Horse emerged from the water, half-dragging Grant.

She scrambled toward them to help White Horse lay Grant on his side on the thin strip of rocky dirt. His eyes were open, but glassy and not focused. His body heaved with every breath.

But at least he was breathing. *Thank you, God.*

THIRTEEN

Faith knelt on one side of Grant as White Horse sank to the ground on the other, his own chest heaving as he caught his breath.

Grant coughed, then turned more fully onto his side as his body ratcheted with a spasm. A second cough came, bringing a squirt of water from his mouth. He coughed once more, then again and again, struggling onto his hands and knees as the fit consumed his body. Splashes of water spewed with some of the heaves.

She could do nothing to help him, so she rested her hands on both of his sides to keep him from toppling with the force of each retch. Had the water entered his lungs? Would it bring on pneumonia or something more permanent?

At last, Grant's coughs subsided, and he sank back onto his side. He'd begun to shiver now, and no wonder, with his clothes soaked with icy river water.

She glanced around them. She should have thought to bring blankets instead of sliding empty-handed down the slope.

"I throw blanket down." White Horse stood, reading her mind. "We camp here. I start fire. Hot water."

She sent him a grateful look. "Thank you. I'll stay with him and help him get warm."

"I'm all right." Grant opened his eyes and moved one arm like he was going to push himself up to sitting. His elbow trembled with that small action.

She laid a hand on the arm. "Rest until we have a blanket. Then you can sit up to wrap in it and get warm."

White Horse strode to the trail she'd used to descend.

Grant's teeth were chattering now, so she scooted closer to wrap her arm over his side. "You can share my warmth until the blanket comes."

His arm dropped against his body, and she half wondered if he would wrap it around her waist, as she was doing with him. Should she recommend he do so? She couldn't quite bring herself to do something so forward, even when he was suffering from such cold.

She didn't breathe much as she waited for White Horse to call from overhead. She was practically hugging Grant, after all. They'd never been this close, not for anything longer than the second it took him to save her that day they first met.

Maybe that was a memory that would distract him from his misery. She smiled. "This reminds me of that first time I saw you, when you helped me at the waterfall."

He let out a hoarse chuckle that turned into a wheeze.

Perhaps best he didn't speak, so she offered another comment. "It seems the two of us aren't very safe around water."

He didn't offer a response, and she couldn't see his face from this angle. Should she find something else to say?

A call from above saved her the struggle. "Blanket."

She scrambled to her feet and moved to catch the coverlet as it fluttered down. This was one of Grant's wool counterpanes that looked like the kind men purchased in St. Louis when they outfitted themselves to go west.

White Horse appeared again with another, this time a folded fur from his own belongings. She stepped to the side so she wasn't under the heavy elk skin, but caught it with her outstretched hands. "Thank you."

With her arms full, she turned back to Grant. He sat up, leaning against the rock wall, and reached for them. He looked more alert now, though his wet hair stuck out in odd angles.

She handed him the wool blanket and helped him wrap it around his shoulders. Then she draped the warm fur over his legs.

"Thanks." His voice was still hoarse from the coughing. Or maybe something worse. Could pneumonia set in this quickly?

She sank down beside him, facing him as he leaned back against the rock wall, his legs stretched before him. This stretch of the path was just wide enough that his feet didn't dangle into the river.

He met her gaze with an exhausted look that he might have meant as a smile, but his jaw still trembled from the cold. It looked like he was clamping his teeth to keep them from chattering.

She leaned forward to pull the blanket more securely around his shoulders so it covered his front too. "What made you jump into the water?" She was too near to meet his gaze, so she focused on the blanket.

"I didn't jump. I was pushed."

She froze, taking in the words. He couldn't mean . . . She drew back and studied his face, met his gaze so close the gold flecks glimmered amidst the green of his eyes. "Pushed?"

Did he mean his horse nudged him from behind? She'd been the only one standing next to him, and she hadn't touched him.

But his gaze hardened, and his jaw tensed even more. He looked away from her, toward the rushing river. "Someone came from behind and slammed into me with both hands. I only caught a glimpse of black shirt as I went over the cliff."

Her chest tightened, her breath stalling. But she managed enough air to shout upward, "White Horse!" Her voice came out unsteady, more high-pitched than she intended.

He heard her, for he replied from above, "Yes?"

She swallowed to strengthen her tone. "Grant said someone pushed him into the river."

White Horse's expression darkened. He didn't speak for long moments, just turned slowly as his gaze searched the land around them. At last, he glanced down again. "Stay until I come back."

Faith nodded. "We'll stay down here."

White Horse disappeared from the edge above, and she settled in to wait. This would give Grant time to regain his strength.

It was hard to keep from looking at him. Hard to keep from worrying about what might have happened to him in the water—both the possible outcomes that could have happened in such a quick-flowing rocky river and also the potential long-lasting effects that might still come.

"Does your chest hurt?" She studied his face for signs of pain.

"Nah." Grant stared out at the river behind her.

"Are you able to breathe fully?"

He cut her a look that said she was being annoying. "Yes."

His grumpiness made her want to press harder, just to bring a smile to the tight line of his mouth. "Are you getting warm? How about your hands and feet? The extremities can be much harder to heat than the rest of you."

He let out a noise that rumbled suspiciously like a growl as he turned to fully look at her. Those thick brows pulled down in a scowl. "Sometimes a man doesn't want to be coddled. Sometimes he'd rather a woman look at him like he's still capable of taking care of himself. And not just himself. Of her and anyone else around too."

She sank back, his tone shaking her confidence a little. But as his words drifted back through her mind, she couldn't help but grin. He'd called her a woman.

Which she was. But Grant hadn't spoken of her that way since . . . well, since he discovered her true identity that second day on the trail.

As though he could read her mind, his eyes darkened, turning emerald with intensity, the air between them thick with . . . could it possibly be desire? Grant swallowed hard, the knob at his throat working.

Her insides curled, and longing burned through her. Would he ever want to lean forward and kiss her? She would do the leaning if that made it easier on his exhausted body.

"Faith, I . . ." He spoke in a voice so rough, his words were barely understandable. He hesitated, studying her as if unsure whether he should continue.

She should say something to encourage him. "Grant,

117

I . . ." But the words jumbled in her mind. "I don't . . . I don't want . . ."

That wasn't right. She *did* want. She gave her head a little shake. "I mean I do. I do wish . . . But I—"

Her words seemed to close off something inside him, and he pulled back. Disappointment sluiced through her, nearly stealing the strength from her body. Why had she said that? Should she tell him she'd not meant to stop him?

But his expression turned guarded. "I need to tell you something, Faith. I think it's better if I speak plain."

FOURTEEN

G rant's heart still raced from how close he'd come to kissing her. He'd stopped himself, though. Or rather, she'd stopped him.

Just in time.

Now he owed her an explanation. She wouldn't understand unless he told her his story.

Told her everything.

Her deep blue eyes drew him like a moth to a flame. He wanted to turn away but couldn't find the strength.

"Faith." His voice barely sounded above the flow of the river. He cleared his throat to give it more strength. "I can't let there be anything . . . between us."

His words hung heavy in the air between them. She held his gaze, searching. She would never guess what all he had to tell her.

The words lodged in his throat like a stone. But as he looked into her eyes, the strength he needed lay glistening there.

He inhaled a steadying breath. "There's so much you don't know about me. For one, I was married."

She didn't even gasp, but he could no longer meet her gaze. He turned to look at the water. "She died nearly two years ago." Almost the length of time they'd been married.

Poor Gloria. She'd deserved so much better than him. He'd done his best to make himself worthy of her. To make her proud. To satisfy her with the life she'd always known and loved.

That line of thought always brought pain, so he pulled his focus back to the facts. "Her liver stopped working. It all happened so fast. She sometimes felt unwell, more so that last year. But she didn't let it slow her down. She lived for her social calendar, even in a frontier city like St. Louis.

"And then, at a party one night, she began casting up her accounts in the retiring room, and she couldn't stop. I hadn't escorted her that night. Her father went in my stead. I was an assistant with the solicitor's office her father started, and one of the partners had a big court proceeding the next day. I was the man who did all the research, laid out the arguing points."

He swallowed down the burn that rose when he remembered that time. Those hard years when he'd worked endlessly to prove himself but never managed to measure up. "Her father brought her home, and the doctor arrived soon after. Two days later, Gloria had faded to a sallow, frail version of herself. She barely had the strength to lift a cup of tea, and then she couldn't keep down what she drank."

He fought to push through the images his mind brought back. "Her father was furious. Demanded Doctor Scott tell him exactly what had caused her liver to fail. The doctor handled him well, better than most men did when Malcolm Sistaire raised his temper. He said liver failure could be caused by many things. Childhood illness that left undetected damage. Genetic predisposition. Ongoing consumption of alcohol. Certain poisons."

He summoned a shrug. "My father-in-law decided poison was the only possibility from that list, and he had me arrested for poisoning my wife. The police were waiting for me when I arrived home from her graveside service."

Faith did emit a slight gasp this time. "Grant." Then her voice gentled. "You weren't to blame for her death."

He kept his gaze fixed on the ground. "Her parents thought so. When it became clear their charge of poisoning wouldn't stand in court, they accused me of not caring for her properly, of neglecting her needs." He swallowed hard against the lump in his throat. His fingers dug into the earth beneath him, desperate for some semblance of grounding in this moment of vulnerability.

"I'm so sorry for your loss. The loss of your wife, and the abandonment of her family when you needed them most." Her words hung in the air, rising above the sound of the flowing water.

He didn't need Mr. and Mrs. Sistaire. Their turning against him had been almost a relief. He could leave that life without feeling like he owed them anything. Yet talking about all this—remembering it all—brought the weight of those days pressing down on his chest, making it hard to breathe.

He looked up at Faith, and her eyes locked with his, their depths reflecting the sincerity behind her words. Her gaze never wavered, just kept an openness that soothed the raw wounds that had festered for so long.

She was far too special for him. He didn't deserve the

way she seemed to still care about him, despite learning this dark part of his past.

She dipped her chin. "What happened next?"

He sent her a grim smile. "It took the court four months to decide I was telling the truth and acquit me. By then, I only wanted to leave St. Louis. That city had been nothing but a bad memory my entire life. It took a while, but I finally found the family who had adopted my little brother. Mrs. Sheldon had died, and Mr. Sheldon said I'd missed Will by one year."

He didn't say the words he'd thought so often since then. *If only I'd tried harder before.* He'd promised Will he'd find him. Why had it taken him fourteen years to make good on his vow?

He let out a breath. "I needed the journey west anyway. The farther we go, the more I leave St. Louis behind." He met her glassy gaze. "I've been able to start fresh." His words made it sound like he intended to build this new life *with her.* He couldn't leave her thinking so.

His throat tightened, but he forced out what he had to say. "But no matter how much I want my past to disappear, it can't. I've lost everyone I've ever loved. I don't have it in me to go through that again."

Faith's eyes rimmed red, and she reached for him. Her hand was a combination of softness and calluses, like the woman herself. Innocent and courageous. Not so naïve of this country that she didn't know the perils, but not afraid to face those dangers for a cause worthy of her determination.

"Grant." Her voice trembled a little. "You've had so many tragedies in your past. I understand why you'd hesitate to allow the chance for loss again. But I hope you won't close yourself off forever. To friendship, if nothing else. You're a good man, and any person would be honored to know you."

She gripped his hand tighter. "*I'm* honored to know you. So many times you've set aside your own comfort and safety to help others. You're wise, savvy, and honest. You kept my secret even when you didn't agree with my choices. You've helped me with my search even when it will delay your own." Her brows rose, a playful glimmer touching her gaze. "You even left the protection of your traveling companions because you weren't sure I'd be safe with a strange Indian man."

He grimaced. White Horse had proven his character more than once since then. He was capable and willing to protect Faith. And he'd saved Grant's life.

Still . . . safety wasn't the only thing Grant had worried about when she said she was leaving with the brave. He wrinkled his nose. "It wasn't so much your protection as your reputation that troubled me enough that I had to come along."

Faith laughed. A surprising sound that caught him off guard with its freedom. She ended with a grin that flashed white teeth. "There's no one out here to worry over my reputation. And if there were, you think they'd be any happier to have me traipsing about in the wilderness— unchaperoned—with *two* men instead of one?"

He pressed his lips. That was a valid point he wasn't ready to concede.

She shrugged the concern away. "Anyhow, White Horse is like a brother in every way except a blood tie." Then her expression sobered, softening. "Please don't close yourself off to friendship. We have an important search ahead of us—two of them. I suspect I, for one, will need a good friend to make sure I don't miss anything important."

He swallowed. She was offering an olive branch. A chance for them to carry on as they had been, maybe.

He should agree. He simply had to make sure he didn't let himself think of her in any way other than as a companion on the journey. A feat that had become harder with each day they spent together. But this was his only option, for he wouldn't abandon her to her search. He couldn't.

So he dipped his chin. "You're right."

She gave her own decisive nod and pushed to her feet. "Are you feeling ready to climb up the slope? There's work to be done."

The morning sun filtered through the pine needles, dappling the ground with light. Faith breathed in the fresh scent of the trees as she rolled up her bedding.

Beside her, Grant grunted as he lifted both their saddles and carried them toward the horses. His eyes were bloodshot, his face drawn. Clearly, he hadn't slept well. Because of his near-drowning?

As her mind brought back the memories from the day before, her chest ached with all the details he'd shared while they sat at the water's edge. So much pain he'd experienced. As if being orphaned and separated from his brother wasn't enough, he'd lost his wife, then her parents turned against him. No wonder he'd turned grumpy and standoffish.

She slung her pack over her shoulder, wincing at the familiar ache in her back. Shouldn't she be accustomed to the rigors of the trail by now?

This would all be worth any pain or hardship once they found Steps Right and finally accomplished Papa's request. The ache in her heart would ease, this pain from knowing she'd not fulfilled what he wanted most—what he'd begged of her specifically.

She reached the horses and strapped her pack behind her saddle. White Horse had already finished with his own mount and was fastening the bridle on her gelding.

"You ready?" Grant led his saddled horse toward them.

She nodded. "I was ready yesterday."

He cracked the first hint of a grin she'd seen all day. A snort slipped from White Horse, but he moved to his own mount.

When they'd all settled in their saddles, White Horse motioned Grant toward the path along the cliff bank. "You ride first. I watch back trail."

The reminder of what happened to Grant yesterday twisted a knot in her belly as they started forward. Who could have possibly pushed him into the river? It seemed so outrageous, not only that someone could have crept up behind them while they were all three standing there, but that there was another person in this wilderness at all. They'd not seen a soul since leaving Parson's group.

And someone who wanted to hurt him enough to push him over the cliff?

She would have believed it his imagination or a tale he created to excuse clumsiness, except he'd also been attacked that night when he stood watch. He'd been by himself then.

The thought that slipped in made her middle coil even more. He wouldn't have made that up. Would he?

He'd been injured. He couldn't have done that to himself.

The water flowed steadily on their left in the canyon far below, and beyond the river rose a craggy slope that followed the water's edge like a wall. Birds chirped in the trees on their right, and the fresh scent of new morning filled the air. It seemed impossible that anything awful might linger in this beautiful land.

Certainly not a stranger trying to hurt them.

As they maneuvered along the water's edge, the sun gradually rose above them. Sometimes they passed through trees that shaded, but on the other side, the heat sweltered even more. At last, they crested a rise in the trail, and in the distance, the sound of rushing water grew louder.

Faith's heart leapt. That had to be a waterfall, though she couldn't see it yet. Maybe they were nearing the end of their journey. Maybe Steps Right was just ahead.

She glanced back at White Horse, and he spared her a quick look and a half smile before returning his focus to the river ahead. She turned forward again and nudged Two Bit faster, pulling alongside Grant.

They were all three riding side by side when she first saw the dip in the water's surface that signaled the top of the falls.

She strained for any sign of a cave or another person in the area. They couldn't yet see the cascading water, but the roar of its flow rose too loud to hear each other speak.

As they came to the edge of the expanse of tumbling liquid, she saw the river was wide here, creating a massive falls that plunged far down into a deep pool. Mist cast a breathtaking rainbow in the sunlight.

She glanced over at Grant to see his reaction. He must have felt her notice, for he turned to her with bright eyes. They spoke a silent question, *Beautiful, isn't it?*

She couldn't help a grin that offered her response. *Incredible.* Part of the weight in her chest had lifted, as if the power of the water had cleared away her worries.

White Horse slipped from his mount, then left the animal as he moved down the steep slope on foot. Looking for a cave behind the falls, no doubt. She slid off her own gelding, and Grant joined her as they maneuvered on foot down the slippery rocks to catch up with him.

As they descended, the mist billowed around them, making it difficult to see more than a few feet ahead. The sound of the water was deafening. She clung to Grant's arm for balance, his nearness igniting warmth that spread up her arm.

White Horse had nearly disappeared from sight, and she struggled to keep up with Grant's quick pace. Finally, they reached the base of the falls, where the pool of water looked dark through the mist.

White Horse had completely disappeared.

FIFTEEN

F aith squinted through the cascade to see if White
Horse had stepped behind the falling water. He must
have. There was no other place where he could have
disappeared to.

"White Horse?" Grant's deep voice barely rose above
the roar of the falls.

Her heart surged a little faster, her skin prickling. Something was wrong.

Grant raised a hand for her to stay, then pulled his arm
from her hold and started forward. If he thought she would
wait here while he found White Horse—and possibly Steps
Right—he was quite mistaken.

The mist had soaked through her clothes, and the shade
of the cliff cooled the air enough to send a shiver through
her as she followed him. When Grant reached the place
where the falling water met the cliff bank, he glanced back
at her with a frown.

She was only a step behind, and she raised her brows
to smile at him. He must have realized trying to keep her

back was a hopeless cause, for he turned again to the falls and pointed to something she couldn't yet see.

She moved to his side, gripping his arm for balance, then sucked in a breath as she caught sight of what he had. A flat stone ledge ran behind the water. A bit of packed mud had been pressed flat in one spot. Someone had walked through here. Many times.

She grinned at Grant, and he met her look. The sparkle in his eyes showed he felt the same way she did. This might finally be the place where they would find Steps Right.

He shifted his arm so he could take her hand, wrapping it tightly in his as he moved toward the narrow path. They slipped under the thin curtain at the edge of the falling water, and she blinked to clear the droplets from her lashes. Behind the falls was much dimmer than outside, and this ledge was barely wide enough for her feet to stand side by side.

The path widened as they advanced toward the middle of the falls, but in the shadows, she couldn't tell if there was a cave or not. Grant's grip on her hand tightened, and she peered around him to better see what he saw. "What is it?"

He probably didn't hear her, for he stepped forward again, pulling her to the widest part of the path. There, just beyond the mist, loomed a dark opening in the rock.

Her heart hammered as Grant released her hand and drew the pistol from his waistband. She should have thought to bring her rifle. Was White Horse already in there? Had he found his mother?

Her hand crept up to the leather strap at her neck. She'd hung the pouch that held the bead necklace on a leather strap around her neck, then tucked it under her shirt. Should she give the gift to Steps Right immediately? Or wait until they'd spoken with the woman, maybe in a special ceremony after they shared a meal?

First, they had to find her. Then maybe she'd know the next step.

They paused at the cave entrance, but inside was thick darkness. It didn't seem to bother Grant, for he stepped forward, pulling her with him. The air smelled dank and musty, but also held a faint scent of herbs.

As her eyes adjusted to the darkness, she could identify the outline of Grant's broad shoulders. She followed close behind, still gripping his hand as he moved deeper into the cave. The scent of herbs mingled with the dank smell of the cave, and a faint glow appeared in the distance.

A campfire?

"Hello?" Grant's voice echoed through the cave. "White Horse?"

A figure appeared in the dim light ahead, though she could barely make out the shape of a person.

"I am here."

Her tension eased at White Horse's familiar voice, and she stepped forward around Grant. "Have you found her?"

He turned, and maybe he motioned them forward, though it was hard to tell in the semidarkness. "Come."

A thrill slipped through her, and she gripped Grant tighter as they walked toward the light. She moved with careful steps, but the crunch of small rocks beneath her shoes sounded loud in the muffled hush of the cave. The faint glow of the campfire flickered against the rough-hewn walls, casting shadows that seemed to come alive the closer they approached.

White Horse moved with certainty, his familiar silhouette a reassuring presence in the strange surroundings. As they approached the fire, her gaze finally found the small woman sitting on the far side. The flames lit her face, shadows deepening the lines carved by her years. Her eyes took them in with a quiet curiosity as they approached.

Steps Right.

They'd finally found her. A knot of emotion clogged Faith's throat.

White Horse moved to stand beside the woman, and his voice held a richness that reverberated through Faith's chest. "My mother. Steps Right."

He turned and spoke to her in the Peigan tongue, slowing as he pronounced Faith's and Grant's names.

Steps Right studied her son as he spoke, then turned again to scan Faith and Grant.

Now was the time. But what should she say to this woman she'd searched for for so long? She should have planned her words, but she didn't have that option now. Maybe best to start by explaining who she was.

Faith took a step forward, her heart rushing once more. "Steps Right. I am so honored to meet you. I'm the daughter of a man you once helped. My father is—was—Martin Collins. You found him injured on the plain and stayed with him, caring for him until help could come."

Maybe she should wait to give her the necklace until they'd visited for a while. Make a real ceremony of it.

For now, she could tell Steps Right what her kindness had meant to Papa. To them all. "He was always grateful for you. We all are. He told us the story many times about how you saved his life."

Steps Right watched her face while she spoke, and even after. Had she understood her words? White Horse had said his mother spoke English. In truth, she'd become so accustomed to White Horse's abilities with the language, she'd not thought about choosing easier words for his mother. If he was concerned his mother might not comprehend what she'd said, he would translate for her.

But then Steps Right nodded. "I remember I find your father." Her voice quavered, but it also held a strength that made Faith want to settle in and listen. "Many winters past, on hunting ground. Find white man hurt. Sun near to sleep. He would not live in cold and dark. My sister get help. I make fire. Keep white man live until sun wake. Tell stories."

A knot formed in Faith's throat. She remembered the things Papa had told her. The stories. A warm tingle spread through her. This was why Faith had worked so hard, to hear these memories.

The old woman paused, her gaze distant as she journeyed back in time. "His woman and his *ookonaa*." She looked to White Horse and squinted, maybe trying to think of the English word.

White Horse murmured something Faith couldn't make out.

Steps Right nodded, then turned back to Faith. "Daughters. Two daughters. He tell of ride horses. Sing. Happy." Her eyes glistened with a smile. "Love woman. Love daughters."

Faith's eyes stung. The two daughters had been Rosemary and Juniper. She and Lorelei hadn't been born yet. She'd known that. But this stark reminder that he'd only spoken of his love for his two eldest stung, no matter how ridiculous the feeling. If she and Lor had been alive then, he would have told stories about them too, surely.

A moment of silence passed before Steps Right continued. "Tell of babe to come. He want to see. Love." She pressed a fist over her heart. "Love babe to come. Not yet born."

Lorelei. Mama must have told him she was with child before he left.

Steps Right's gaze refocused, meeting Faith's again. "Is you?"

Another rush of emotion slammed into her, pressing her chest and searing her eyes and nose. She shook her head. "My sister Lorelei." The words came out a hoarse whisper. She'd been the only one not mentioned.

She was being petty and unreasonable. Her father hadn't spoken of her because he'd had no knowledge he would have a fourth daughter. She'd always hated being the baby, but this had to be the worst of all outcomes.

White Horse spoke to his mother in their tongue, his voice low and rhythmic and far too quick for her to understand. He'd taught them a few words in his language, but she could catch nothing now. Not even while watching their expressions.

Steps Right looked earnest as she answered, but that could mean any number of things.

Grant took a quiet step to stand beside her, as though he understood this insecurity that unsteadied her. His presence was a solid, comforting force, a rock in the midst of these whirling emotions. She allowed her upper arm to lean against his, drawing strength from his support.

Finally, White Horse turned back to them, his face serious. The firelight lit his cheek, casting his dark eyes in shadows. "My mother hides." He paused, his jaw hardening. "Hides from Flies Ahead. Grandson of chief."

Faith frowned at his words. They had met Flies Ahead and his grandfather, Son of Owl, back when she and her sisters first came west to the rendezvous and Riley helped them search for Steps Right. Neither Flies Ahead nor his grandfather had been helpful in their search, and the younger man had seemed especially untrusting. And untrustworthy.

White Horse shifted, and the firelight showed a flash of anger in his eyes. "Send warriors to find her three times." He held up as many fingers.

The revelation hung heavy in the air, the gravity of the situation sinking in. They'd known Steps Right had been forced to leave her village—the home and friends she'd lived with her entire life—when one of her patients had died, despite her care. That patient had been Flies Ahead's father, the man who would have become chief when his father, Son of Owl, died. Apparently, Flies Ahead hadn't been satisfied with the punishment of sending an old woman out into the wilderness by herself. He'd decided to hunt her down too.

Faith studied White Horse as that thought settled in a different way. "Why would he search for her? He was the one who sent her away."

"His *grandfather* make her leave." White Horse was doing a remarkable job holding back his anger, though it sounded in his voice. "Flies Ahead gone when happen. Go to mountains to . . ." He searched for the word he wanted and found it quickly. "Grieve. For father no more."

The situation was becoming far clearer, and her own belly churned with anger too. "So Flies Ahead returned from his time of mourning and found that the woman he wanted vengeance from had been sent away."

White Horse didn't answer, though the anger simmering in him tightened the air around them.

She couldn't blame him. His mother had been living in fear, hiding in caves from a danger that he knew nothing about. She hadn't even turned to her son for help like White Horse had been certain she would. He worked so hard to protect those he deemed friends. Learning this must bring both grief and anger.

The fire crackled softly, the only sound in the heavy silence. Would White Horse go back to his old village? Would he confront Flies Ahead? Fight him?

As if Steps Right was thinking the same thing, she spoke to him in Peigan, her gaze intense. She seemed to be instructing, or maybe trying to convince him of something.

White Horse answered in the same terse tone as before. Then silence reigned once again.

Faith had more questions, though she wondered if it would stir his anger more to voice them. If she didn't ask now, she might not have another chance. "How did Flies Ahead know where you went? Did he find you, or did you see him before he found you?"

Steps Right's eyes reflected the firelight. "Not find me. Warriors come. I see. I move. Not find me."

She must have decided they'd spoken enough of her plight, for she motioned to the ground around the fire. "Sit. Eat." She reached for a wooden bowl placed close to the fire. White Horse sometimes used the same kind of dish to cook with in his lodge.

They moved to sit by the fire, with Faith settling between

Grant and White Horse. Grant had been quiet through the conversation, maybe thinking he was an outsider when it came to what they'd been discussing.

She glanced over at him. She wanted him to be a part of this. He'd been by her side through nearly this entire journey, after all.

The fire illuminated his face and the wet shirt that clung to his shoulders and chest, outlining the strength there. Her own damp clothing held a chill that made the fire's warmth a welcome relief.

As Steps Right passed dishes of stew, a rich aroma rose above the scent of the campfire. Faith lifted her bowl and held it in front of her mouth as she breathed in. "This smells wonderful."

Steps Right smiled, more with her eyes than her mouth. But her pleasure was impossible to miss.

As Faith took her first sip of broth, the savory flavor was unlike anything she'd tasted. A symphony of tastes, a testament to Steps Right's skill with herbs and spices.

While they ate, White Horse and Steps Right spoke in their language. Faith couldn't understand the words, but she caught the shift of concern on White Horse's face. He seemed to ask a few more questions, then turned to Faith and Grant. "My mother is hurt." He pointed to her ankle. "Hard to walk."

Concern pressed in Faith's chest, and she turned to Steps Right. "What happened? What can we do to help you?" Yet Steps Right was the healer among them. Was there anything more that she'd not been able to do on her own?

The older woman shook her head. "I fall. Need sit. Heal."

Maybe a sprained ankle, then. Faith studied the woman's

foot, but the way she had it positioned, her buckskin dress covered most of the appendage.

She looked back up at Steps Right. "We'll make sure you get all the rest you need. If there's anything you want, just ask one of us."

Steps Right returned a kind look but didn't seem to want to say more.

White Horse spoke up, though. "We take my mother back to the ranch. Soon."

She met his gaze. He likely wanted to get her to a safe place, away from Flies Ahead. At the ranch, Steps Right could rest, and Faith and her sisters could help her. "When do you want to leave? Tomorrow?" That felt too soon, though. Grant hadn't found his brother.

White Horse shook his head. "Rest tomorrow. Then leave."

The day after tomorrow, then. She slid a quick look to Grant, but his expression was hard to read.

She reached for the used dishes and stacked them. "I'll take these to the water for washing." She needed a few minutes alone to think about this deluge of new information and churning emotions.

"I'll get the horses settled where they can graze." Grant pushed to his feet.

She straightened. "I forgot about the horses. I'll help you first, then wash the dishes." White Horse would likely want time alone with his mother anyway.

They made their way back to the cave's entrance, and she followed Grant along the narrow path behind the waterfall. When they stepped out from behind the curtain of water, the sun's heat pressed down in stark contrast to the cool dampness of the cave. She placed the dishes beside the water, then followed him up the slope to the horses.

The horses grazed quietly on the rocky hillside, still wearing their saddles and packs. She stayed at Grant's side as he approached his mount first. While he rubbed the gelding's head, she stroked the sweat-dampened shoulder, eyeing Grant.

His expression looked troubled, and he surely realized she wanted to talk with him. At last, he looked her way, and she took the opportunity.

"If we start back the day after tomorrow, what will you do?"

He continued stroking the flat part of the gelding's head, but the wrestling in Grant's spirit clouded his gaze. "I guess I'll ride with you to your ranch. See that Steps Right gets there safely. Then I'll start looking for Will again."

Her own spirit twisted, conflicted. Grant would see the ranch. Meet her sisters. She wouldn't have to say good-bye to him so soon. But he would have to delay his own search. And then he would be all alone in this wilderness.

Two Bit gave a soft nicker, calling her over to him. For now, she could let Grant's words stand. Maybe a better way would become clear.

She approached Two Bit and rubbed his head while he snuffled her hand. "Sorry, boy. So much has happened, I couldn't come back to you right away."

She rubbed his neck and stared out at the flowing river where it gathered speed to cascade over the falls. The mountains rose beyond, majestic yet treacherous.

She had achieved what she and her sisters set out to do more than three years before. She'd accomplished what Papa asked. But the longing inside her hadn't eased.

Was it simply the fact that Papa hadn't been able to speak of Faith to Steps Right all those years ago that bothered her so much? That was too silly to be the real reason, but maybe it was a symptom of her deeper problem. Her mind felt too muddled just now to figure it out.

A warm wind kicked up, brushing the hair from her face. Maybe getting Steps Right back to the ranch would help. Perhaps with those final pieces of the journey, she would find the peace she so desperately craved.

SIXTEEN

Only the faint hint of light from the direction of the cave opening gave Grant a clue that morning might have come at last. The hard stone floor had offered little comfort, but that probably wasn't the only reason he'd struggled to stay asleep.

White Horse rose quietly from his bedding and padded out of the cave. Grant sat up too and glanced toward Steps Right. The older woman's even breathing continued, which was good. She probably needed the rest.

Near her, Faith stirred, then sat upright, her hand moving to the leather cord she wore around her neck. The soft light of the fire gave her an angelic glow, and her sleep-rumpled hair made her look so adorable. When she sent a tired smile toward him, his heart quickened.

Keeping himself from falling for her was becoming harder each day.

Perhaps he shouldn't help them take Steps Right back to the ranch. He was much closer to Will from this point. And White Horse would be capable of protecting the women. Faith would be there to see to her injury and needs.

Faith was already rising, moving to the cooking supplies. He'd noticed when he helped put things away last night that their stock of meat was getting low. This morning would be a good time to hunt, while the animals were out enjoying the cool air and the safety of the fog that often spread through the valleys.

He straightened his blankets, then pulled on his boots and rose as White Horse came back into the cave. Grant checked his rifle, then reached for his possibles sack to make sure he had enough bullets and powder.

Faith moved close enough to whisper. "What are you doing?"

"Going hunting." He secured the clasp on the bag and looped the strap over his neck.

"Can I come too?"

He met her gaze, which held far too much pleading. "Why?"

She glanced toward the cave opening. "It would be nice to get out."

He could certainly agree with that. Living in this darkness felt like a heavy blanket pressing on his chest. And if he decided not to accompany them to the ranch, this might be his last day with Faith before they went their separate ways. He would have to talk with her about that, but first, they could enjoy a final ride together. "Can you be ready soon?"

She nodded but didn't smile as she normally did. Was something bothering her? "I'm ready now." She looked to White Horse. "Will you be here with your mother?"

He'd settled against the back wall with his knife and the block of wood he'd started carving into a bowl last night. He looked up at her now and nodded.

Within minutes, Grant led Faith from the cave, along the ledge, then onto the bank and up the slope. The horses were already grazing in the cool morning air, so he and Faith quickly saddled and mounted, then started down a path that followed the river away from the falls.

As they rode, quiet settled between them. The undisturbed calm of the morning made it easier not to speak. But every time he looked toward Faith, the lines pressing her brow showed her mind was already churning.

What concerns muddled her thoughts so early in the morning? If there was anything he could do to ease her mind, he would. That would take his mind off the need to make a firm decision about leaving her.

As their path left the water's edge and wove through the pines, their horses were able to walk side by side. He took the chance to speak. "What do you think about Steps Right's situation?" He slid a glance toward her before focusing again on the trail. Hopefully a deer would wander from the trees, and he had to be ready.

Faith took a moment before responding, and when she did, her voice carried the same tension she wore on her face. "I'm worried." She paused, but then continued. "If we take Steps Right back to my sisters' ranch, will she be safe there, or will she bring the danger with her? Will White Horse go find Flies Ahead and end the threat once and for all? White Horse is a strong warrior, but against an entire village . . . ?"

His question had released a dam. Like water tumbling over the falls, her words spewed out one after the other. "How will we manage the ranch without him? He's a partner, after all. And he accomplishes nearly as much work as the rest of us combined. Maybe we could handle things for a while, but when Juniper and Lorelei have their babies, I'm not sure Rosie, Riley, and I can do the training and everything else required."

Her voice dropped even lower. "And Steps Right's ankle . . . is it only a sprain? How long will it take to mend? Is it only rest she needs, or something else? Could it be broken? If so, should we splint it before we start back to the ranch?"

The turmoil in her expression made his chest ache. He reined his horse closer to hers, reaching out to take her hand.

She lifted her brows at him, but then gave an effort toward a smile as she clasped his hand. That was Faith—smiling no matter how hard her struggle.

He gave a gentle squeeze. "We'll figure things out. Give it a little more time."

They found no deer after a half hour, so he turned them back toward the falls. Yet by the time they rode the horses up the slope to the grassy area at the top of the falls where White Horse's animal was tied, Grant couldn't bring himself to return to the darkness.

They tied their geldings to graze, then he pulled his rifle from the saddle and turned to walk to the river's edge. The water flowed faster here, rushing to cascade over the falls. The wind ruffled his hair, easing the unrest in his spirit.

Beyond the river, the mountains rose in rocky peaks, a few of the taller ones still spotted with snow in some of their crags. Before coming west, he'd never imagined a land could hold this much beauty, such a richness that captivated him.

"Do you want to walk upriver with me?" Faith's voice

broke through his thoughts. The sound of it soothed him even more, yet her nearness tightened something in his middle.

She was such a beautiful woman, even after days on the trail. But it wasn't just her beauty that had become harder to resist with each passing day. She was so strong. So courageous. She made him want to be the same.

Made him want to open himself to love again. To risk the chance of loss and pain, for the possibility that they might *not* face those burdens. At least not for a long time. That they could experience joy and contentment.

But that was still the problem. When you loved someone, eventually that person would be wrenched away from you. Either now or when you were both gray and wrinkled—or any moment in between.

He couldn't stand another stripping away of everything he loved most.

He shook his head to dispel the thoughts. He couldn't let himself touch her. Especially if they were parting ways tomorrow. He had to keep his distance, had to keep his feelings in check.

She was still waiting for his answer, so he turned and started a slow walk upstream. She fell into step beside him. Thankfully, she left enough space between them their arms wouldn't accidentally brush. Still, his mind whirled with her nearness.

After a minute, Faith spoke. "What's your favorite memory with Will, besides when you two would look at stars?"

He slid a glance at her. That was a harder question than she might think. He had to think back, way back, to a different life. When he still had people who loved him. When the weight of the world hadn't yet settled on his shoulders.

A memory surfaced, a glimpse of a time he'd long ago forced from his thoughts. Bringing it back now felt like glass scraping his skin. But he forced himself. For Faith.

"We used to sneak into a neighbor's field, Will and me." He cleared his throat. "We would pretend to be wild horses, galloping around. I was always the lead stallion, and Will was my loyal follower. Sometimes we raced. I was faster, of course, since I was older. But when Will got frustrated, I let him win instead. We spent hours out there, running and laughing until our sides hurt."

He could almost feel the Missouri grass beneath his feet, could almost hear Will's laughter echoing in his ears. For a moment, he was back in that field, a young boy with dreams as big as the sky, with a brother who was his best friend and partner in any adventure.

For a moment, he was home.

Faith's eyes took on a gentle smile. "Lorelei and I used to pretend we were catching wild horses. She would doctor all their injuries, give them names, and care for them." She slid a look at him. "But I always imagined they were trying to run away from the ranch. I would have to ride after them and bring them back."

The mischievous gleam in her eyes made her so beautiful, he could barely stand the pain in his chest. What a picture she must have been as a girl, her hair flying in the wind while she chased imaginary horses, her laughter echoing through the fields.

They walked in silence another minute, and he worked to pull himself from the spell of that image. Back to the present, with the river flowing over rocks beside them, a woman at his side who understood him like no one else ever had, not even Gloria.

Sometimes it seemed Faith saw the parts of him he did his best to hide. But the biggest wonder was that his weaknesses didn't push her away. Instead, she pressed in harder.

That felt like a miracle . . . if a person believed there was a God who cared.

He slid a look at her as a question wove through his mind. "Do you believe in God?" The moment the words came out, he wanted them back.

Especially when she turned toward him, a curious expression on her face. But her eyes didn't look condescending. Nor shocked. She looked like she was really contemplating her answer.

"I . . ." She hesitated, then gave a single nod. "Yes. I do believe in God."

She'd technically answered the question but told him nothing.

He dipped his chin. "And . . . ?"

She gave him a wry smile. "And . . . my parents took us to church. We prayed at meals. Prayed at bedtime. My sisters are all strong in their faith."

It seemed she wanted him to ask the obvious question, so he did. "And why don't you believe?"

She kept her focus ahead. "I do believe in God." Then she cut her gaze to him. "As I just said." The corners of her mouth twitched, but then she let out a long breath as she stared at the ground ahead. "I've tried, I really have. It's just that . . . I don't *feel* Him the way my sisters do."

When she looked over at him, her eyes begged for understanding. "They talk about Him like He really hears. Like He cares what they say and responds to them. I still ask Him for help when something goes wrong, but . . . I don't know if He doesn't care or if I'm not good at listening. I'm not sure I've ever heard an answer."

He knew exactly what she meant. Neither the Flagstones who took him in after his parents died nor Gloria's family had been religious. But he'd known a few people through the years—like the headmaster at school—who prayed like God really answered them.

He'd tried it once. That day the week before Christmas when he was fifteen, he came home to the Flagstones' home and found it empty. Boarded up, with not even a note saying where they'd gone.

He'd been fighting tears, with no notion what to do or who to ask. He sat down on the outside stairs and prayed the way Headmaster Lawton did. Asking the Almighty to show him what he should do next.

God hadn't answered.

So, Grant had picked himself up—as he always had to do—and went back to school. Headmaster Lawton let him stay for the Christmas holiday, and after a few inquiries, found that the Flagstones had moved to Springfield. They'd not felt it necessary to inform the school, though thankfully they'd already paid the remaining tuition for the spring term.

They hadn't taken the time to send Grant a note either. Not even a simple missive with their new address. They must not have wanted him to know where to find them. They must have wanted to be rid of the orphan boy they'd reluctantly taken in five years before.

He'd spent every moment of those next few months either

studying or working odd jobs. Anything he could do to earn enough for the next year's tuition. If he wasn't allowed to stay at school, he'd have nowhere else to go.

And so went the next three years. By the end, he'd met and begun courting Gloria. They were both young. Too young.

She should have found someone far better than him. Her parents certainly felt so. But once they realized their daughter would accept no other outcome, Mr. Sistaire took Grant into his business. Grant had worked harder during those days than any other time in his life. He *would* prove himself to his future father-in-law.

After he and Gloria were married, her father made him a junior solicitor, with the promise of eventually becoming a partner in the firm.

That all changed the night Gloria came home ill from the party.

"Grant?"

Faith's voice tugged at him, pulling him from the downward swirl of memories. He forced himself to turn to her, his mind grappling for what had last been said.

Her sisters' faith. Right.

He swallowed to bring moisture back into his mouth. He couldn't let Faith become cynical and bitter like he was. She was everything good. Everything he couldn't be.

"Faith." Her blue eyes searched his, and he pressed on. "What your sisters have is real. It can be real for you too. I don't know how to find it, but I think if your heart is open . . . if you ask Him, God will be there. He'll answer you. It might not be in ways you expect, but it will be Him answering."

What madness was he spewing? He didn't even believe

those words—at least they hadn't proven true in his own life. But Faith needed something to cling to. Maybe God would come through for her if she asked Him. She was good enough. Surely.

Her eyes glistened, and she nodded. "Thank you." Then she glanced behind her. "Should we turn back?"

Part of him didn't want to. He'd be happy walking with her the rest of the day, even if she asked hard questions of him. But White Horse and Steps Right would wonder about them. He certainly didn't want them thinking the worst.

As they turned toward the waterfall, Faith must have wanted to lighten the conversation. She sighed, and her voice took on a lighter tone. "I love rivers. The first time I saw *you* was beside a river." She raised a brow as she slid a look at him.

Was she teasing? That was a good sign. Maybe her worries had eased.

He snorted and returned the jab. "I was *pulling* you out of that river."

She wrinkled her nose. "I didn't fall in. I had a firm grip on the rock."

He shrugged. "Your hands might have been wrapped around a stone, but the rest of you dangled over the water. You'd have been swimming in less than a minute if I hadn't shown up."

She tipped her head at him, curiosity slipping into her gaze. "What were you doing there anyway? It was early in the morning."

The memory of that day slipped back through. "I'd come to the falls the night before, trying to get away from all the drinking and noise at the rendezvous. Ended up sleeping there. I saw you come that morning, but I didn't want to disturb you." He cut her a look. "I figured realizing you were alone in such a remote place with a strange man might be alarming."

A smile curved Faith's mouth. "Little did you know that wouldn't worry me overmuch."

A pang twisted in his chest. That was exactly the problem. And it meant he had to worry enough for both of them. Or rather, he needed to stand strong and keep his hands to himself.

But just as he prepared to step away from her, putting more distance between them to clear his head, Faith stopped and turned to him.

He reluctantly did the same. When she fixed those clear blue eyes on his, her earnest gaze seeing all the way to his soul, he couldn't summon enough moisture in his dry mouth to speak.

Her voice started tentatively. "Grant, I . . ." She paused, her throat working. Did her gaze just drop to his lips?

He had to clench his hands to keep from reaching out to pull her close. If only she knew how much she undid him— her words and everything else about her. But he couldn't let her know, or else he'd lose the last remnants of his control.

Her focus flicked up to his eyes again, and he could see her nervousness. Did she feel something for him? He'd thought it before. Maybe. But if it were actually true . . . if she experienced even a thread of the overwhelming pull that gripped every part of him . . .

When her gaze dipped to his mouth again and lingered there, his entire body heated, burning away his resolve. He reached for her . . .

. . . and she came to him.

He cupped her shoulders, savoring her warmth, relishing her beauty, the rich tan on her cheeks that proved her adventurous streak. He lowered his mouth, and she rose up to meet him partway.

Faith fought the nerves in her middle as she pressed her lips to Grant's. But then the warm intensity of his mouth took over, clearing every thought from her mind.

Dear sweet Rosa. This man filled her senses and overwhelmed every one of them. She lifted her hands to his chest, but they wouldn't stay there. They slid up to wrap around his neck, her fingers tangling in his wet hair. The taste of him was intoxicating, mixed with the wild scent of the trees that had brushed against him as they rode, and even a hint of smoke from that morning's campfire.

He slowed the kiss, though she was nowhere near ready to stop. Grant was so much more . . . She couldn't string together enough words to finish that thought.

But the one thing she did comprehend clearly—oh so vividly—was that Grant admired her. As she did him.

He pulled back, just enough to allow them both to breathe. She inhaled gulps of air as his chest heaved too. She couldn't stop the smile that tugged her cheeks wide.

But then he eased a little farther back, enough that she could focus on his eyes. They weren't smiling. In fact, a touch of worry clouded their earnest depths. "I'm sorry if I took liberties I shouldn't have. I didn't mean . . . I don't . . ."

He seemed to be struggling for words, and a flash of

fear rose in her chest at what he might say if she let him continue. So she placed a finger on his lips, silencing him. "Don't apologize, Grant. I wanted that too."

Realization of what she'd just said surged the moment the words left her mouth. Heat flushed through her, and she cringed. "I mean . . ." She pulled back a little, wanting to cover her face with her hands.

He chuckled, and his hands rested on her upper arms, keeping her from going far. "It's nice to know the feeling is mutual."

She dared only a quick glance at his face, but the softness there eased some of her mortification. She let out a long breath, willing the embarrassment away. Letting herself rest in his hold, soaking in the chance to study his face—every handsome feature there.

His expression turned more sober again, but she didn't fear this time. She wanted to know what held him back. They could face it together if they spoke of it.

At last he said, "I told myself I wouldn't get close to anyone again. It's too hard to lose them." He didn't add *but you're worth that risk.* Which meant fear still held him too tightly.

Perhaps he only needed time. She could give him that.

So she pressed a hand to his chest, her palm flat against the warmth that rose through his shirt. She could feel a little of the pounding in his heart too. "We don't have to rush this. There's so much else happening. We can take time to see where we want this to lead."

He paused a moment, as though he wasn't sure he wanted to agree. But then he nodded. "You're right. There's a lot happening." He gave her arms a gentle squeeze, then released her. "You should get back before White Horse comes searching."

Before she could answer, a flash of movement in the trees upriver caught her focus. A deer?

The animal stepped from the brush toward the water, its ears flicking all directions for a threat.

Faith pressed a finger to her lips and pointed past Grant for him to look.

In a second, he'd raised his rifle and aimed. As much as she hated this part, they needed the meat. Their stores were running too low.

Faith turned away, preparing for the blast of the gun.

As Faith stepped into the cave an hour later, she raised her voice to signal her presence. "I've returned." The last thing she wanted was for White Horse to think her an intruder. The yawning darkness ahead swallowed her words, especially with the muffled pounding of the falls behind her.

When she rounded the curve in the corridor, the light of the campfire appeared ahead, and the noise of the water faded to a muffled hum. White Horse was helping his mother settle on the fur that had been her seat the day before.

Faith held up the bundle in her hands. "Grant got a deer. I've brought some of the hind meat, and he'll bring the rest when he's finished dressing it."

"Here." Steps Right motioned to the place beside her where she prepared food. "Make pemmican." She turned to her son and spoke a string of directions in Peigan.

White Horse moved to his packs, probably to retrieve supplies.

Faith crouched beside the woman and laid the meat on the work surface. Steps Right took up her knife as White Horse brought a pouch of dried berries.

Steps Right motioned toward the stone floor beneath Faith. "Sit. Help."

Comfortable silence settled around them while Steps Right began slicing the meat. Her gnarled fingers seemed to struggle with the task, though. There was no need for her to be uncomfortable when Faith sat idle.

"I can do that." Faith shifted forward again.

Steps Right studied her for a moment, then nodded and handed over the knife. "Cut thin. Then dry. Make powder. Add berries. Eat all winter." Faith nodded as she took over the task. White Horse said this food could last for months without spoiling.

As she sliced, her mind wandered to how many times the woman might have made pemmican in her life. Had she learned as a young girl, working with her mother and grandmother? Steps Right's knowledge and skills were a testament to her life and experiences, a legacy of survival and resilience.

The work was methodical—an easy way to lose track of time. The cave, once a place of mystery and uncertainty, now felt like a sanctuary, a place where she was learning not just how to make pemmican but also gaining a deeper understanding of Steps Right and her way of life.

The sound of footsteps echoed through the cave. That was Grant's stride. White Horse and Steps Right must have recognized it too, for neither looked worried about a stranger's approach. He stepped into the firelight, his arms laden with the rest of the deer meat.

"There." Steps Right motioned to where he should place his load. Then she pointed to his spot by the fire. "Sit."

Grant glanced at Faith with raised brows, but she only smiled at him. Steps Right possessed a straightforward manner, but it was refreshing now that she was growing accustomed to it.

As Grant settled on the stone, White Horse rose and strode toward the cave opening. He didn't say where he was going, and Faith almost called out to ask. If he'd wanted her to know, though, he would have said. Finding his mother and learning the truth of her situation might have unsettled him as much as it had Faith.

The fire crackled softly, casting shadows on the cave walls as Steps Right positioned the meat Grant had just brought and Faith began slicing it too.

The older woman broke the silence as she looked at Grant. "Who teach to hunt?" She regarded him as she waited for his answer.

Grant stared at her for a moment. Was he not sure what she meant? But then he spoke. "My father taught me when I was young."

A pang pressed in Faith's chest. No wonder he'd hesitated. Were those good memories? He'd been ten when his parents died, so he couldn't have had much time to learn the skill.

Steps Right nodded and continued to study him. Did she realize the question had probably raised a host of tangled emotions?

A twinkle slipped into her eyes. "My son hunt when young boy. Want father to teach. First hunt, find deer. Walk." She spread her arms wide and mimicked the motion of creeping quietly through the grass. "Ready shoot." She pretended to draw back on a bow. Then she squeezed her eyes shut like she was about to sneeze. "Achoo!" She opened her eyes and grinned. "Deer run. Hunt no good."

Faith chuckled, and even Grant smiled. It wasn't hard to imagine a young White Horse, disappointed and embarrassed by an untimely sneeze. She'd have to tease him about it when she had the chance.

Steps Right smiled in the memory for a long moment, then turned back to Grant. "Why come?" She motioned around them. She probably didn't mean to ask why he'd come to the cave. Maybe why he'd come to this land, so distant from the States?

He raised his brows. "Why did I come west? To this mountain country?"

Steps Right nodded.

Again, sadness touched his eyes. "I'm looking for my brother. Will Sheldon." He added on the last part like an afterthought, maybe to see if Steps Right had heard of him. That didn't seem likely, though.

But she straightened. "Will?" Her voice held pleasure.

"You know him?" Grant leaned forward.

Steps Right nodded. "I find sick. In snow."

Faith's heart had picked up so much speed, she strained to make sure she didn't miss anything over the pounding.

Grant seemed ready to push to his feet and start searching for his brother. But he voiced his questions instead. "When? Is he all right? Where is he?"

The older woman nodded. "I stay in cabin. Give the healing plants. He good man. Ask me to stay there." She shook her head. "I come to cave. Safe here." A twinkle slipped into her eye. "He bring food. Sit and talk."

Energy emanated from Grant's body through the air between them. "What did he say?"

Her gaze took on a distant expression as she looked toward the fire. "He tell when boy. Play in river." She motioned toward the cave opening and the water beyond. "With brother."

Grant nodded. "Yes. Near the mill. We swam and fished there all the time."

She nodded, her expression warming. "He speak of this. Say he fear water. Brother make him brave."

Warmth surged through Faith's chest, so strong it made her eyes burn. Hearing this had to give Grant hope.

He didn't answer for a few heartbeats, but when he did, his voice had gained determination. "Where is he now? I have to find him."

Again Steps Right nodded. "Cabin near river. One day to ride and come back."

Grant rose abruptly, pushing to his feet. "I'm going to see if White Horse needs help." His voice sounded tight, then he turned and strode out of the cave.

Unease churned in Faith's middle. She had to talk to Grant. He would want to go to Will. He was probably planning how to even now. She laid down the knife and meat. "I'll be back in a minute."

Rising, she made her way through the cave passage, then washed her hands in the waterfall. After following the ledge, she jumped to the bank just in time to see Grant's retreating back as he climbed the hill toward the horses. "Grant, wait." She hurried after him.

He stopped and spun around, his face tight. "I have to find Will." He held up his fingers an inch apart. "I'm this close to him. I have to go today. Now."

A wave of panic washed through her. He couldn't go by himself. Should she go with him? But she couldn't, not if she and White Horse were going to leave tomorrow morning to take Steps Right back to the ranch. Would White Horse delay another day?

She sucked in a breath through the weight on her chest. "Wait." Her voice shook a little. "We need to talk to White Horse."

Without a pause, Grant turned and yelled up the hill. "White Horse!" His voice thundered loud enough to rise above the waterfall. Did he know for sure the man was up there?

Apparently so, for White Horse appeared at the top of the hill, his figure silhouetted against the blue sky behind him. He strode toward them, leaping over some of the rocks, his face set in a scowl. When he came close enough, he barked, "Quiet. Do not bring danger."

Grant didn't answer, but he waited for White Horse to reach them before speaking again. "My brother is close." He bit the words. "Your mother said only a half-day's ride away. I have to go find him."

Faith ventured her question. "Could we wait here an extra day? Maybe Grant can find his brother and bring him back here. Then we can all go back to the ranch together." Even as she spoke the words, their naiveté rang in her ears. Who was she to Grant's brother to stop his life and come to the ranch just because she wanted him to? She, a person Will had never met or ever heard of?

White Horse stood silent for a long moment, his gaze shifting between Grant and Faith. His dark eyes were even harder to read now than usual. Then he met Faith's eyes. "I must get my mother to safety." His voice carried the weight of a thousand unspoken words. "She is hurt. Flies Ahead will come again." Then his focus moved to Grant. "We will give you the direction of the ranch. You can come when you are ready."

Grant nodded. "I will." Then he turned toward the slope where the horses grazed at the top. "I have to go. There's no time to waste."

SEVENTEEN

Faith stood with White Horse at the river's edge as the final flash of Grant's horse disappeared through the trees lining the bank.

Her heart ached to go with him. Not to let him leave by himself. She and White Horse had drawn a map for him to the ranch, and she'd encouraged him to bring Will too. He said he would try. But what if Will wouldn't come and Grant decided to stay with his brother? The loss of Grant Allen in her life felt too hard to face.

She drew in a steadying breath. She had to stay the course. Had to focus on Steps Right. Had to trust that Grant would come back to her.

Did she dare ask God for His hand to ensure that happened? She couldn't bring herself to. It seemed a selfish prayer, bothering God with a matter of the heart when He should be focused on much greater things.

"Your heart pulls two ways like river divided by stone." White Horse's deep voice spoke quietly beside her.

Faith nodded, blinking back silly tears. She couldn't let herself be so emotional about this.

"Place him in God's hands. Creator Father will work all for good if you ask Him to."

Faith managed a small smile. "I was just thinking of that." Though her thoughts hadn't been so righteous. *God, if it's not too much to ask, bring Grant to us. To me.*

She sighed, her hand lifting to the cord at her neck as a reminder of her mission. But her fingers didn't feel the rough rawhide of the string holding the pouch of beads. Only the cotton of her dress. She reached higher, then casually slid her hand under the fabric, reaching all the way to her arm as her heart hammered.

She couldn't have lost it.

She tried not to show the panic welling through her as she brushed her hand over the fabric at her waist. Maybe the cord had come untied, and the pouch slipped down in the layers of cloth.

She could feel no bulge under the material, though. White Horse didn't show that he noticed her odd movements, but he probably saw them anyway. She had to get by herself so she could search thoroughly.

She turned back toward the waterfall. "I'm going to check on your mother."

He didn't answer and didn't follow. As she prepared to step onto the first of the rocks that led to the ledge behind the falls, she glanced back to make sure she was alone.

Her pulse hammered as she paused in the cave opening where she would have enough light and room to move around, as well as protection from White Horse's view by the falling water.

She patted the layers of her shirt but could feel nothing out of place. No bulge of leather or line of a rawhide string.

It felt like a weight pressed on her chest, and her fingers trembled as she unfastened buttons. If she'd lost the beads . . . what would her sisters say? What would Papa have said? He would be so disappointed.

She couldn't fail him. Not like this.

But after she'd unfastened, searched, and refastened every piece of clothing, no sign of the pouch or the blue bead necklace had revealed itself.

Tears pressed hard against her eyes, but she couldn't let them fall. She forced herself to breathe, to take in air and think through where she might have lost it.

She'd not removed the pouch from her neck at any point since tying it there before she left the ranch. In fact, she'd made a habit of feeling for the security of the cord each morning when she arose. Had she done so that morning?

Yes. It had definitely been there when she stood to follow Grant out to hunt. And when she'd settled in her saddle on Two Bit, she'd reached to make sure it was secure then also. She couldn't remember feeling for it any time after that.

Had she lost it during the hunt? If not, it would be in the cave. She should check there first, then if she had to, she would retrace every step she'd walked or ridden that day. She had to find the beads. If she'd ruined her chance to accomplish her father's dying wish, she might never find the peace she craved so deeply.

Steps Right was sitting in her usual place, and it looked like she'd been dozing. Faith gave her an apologetic smile. "I'm sorry if I woke you." Then she refocused her gaze on the cave floor where she'd been sitting to make the pemmican.

"What seek?" Steps Right's voice held the quaver of sleep.

Faith swallowed. "A pouch I was wearing around my neck. I think the cord broke." She certainly couldn't tell her what was inside.

There was no sign of the necklace here, so she turned back toward the entrance. "I'm going to look outside." As she maneuvered the dark corridor, she scuffled her feet along the stone floor, feeling for the bag.

Still nothing.

When she reached the grassy bank, she studied the ground as she strode up the hill toward the horses. White Horse must have gone up to the animals already. He'd said he was planning to check their hooves this afternoon.

As she crested the hill, he was just lowering Two Bit's left hind leg. He straightened and turned to watch her, but she kept her focus on the ground, though she could feel his gaze.

She would have to tell him. What would he do? If he told his mother she'd lost the beads . . . the heirloom that so many generations of her family had treasured and worked so hard to protect . . . She couldn't breathe, so she pushed that thought aside.

He wouldn't show his anger. He would be fair. And he would help look. They had to find it before they left this place tomorrow morning.

She made herself walk toward him, though she scanned the ground with each step. At last, she halted at Two Bit's head and stroked the gelding's face as she gathered her courage.

"I . . . I've lost the blue bead necklace." She swallowed down the lump that blocked more words. "Your mother's necklace. I had it in a pouch tied around my neck. It was still there when I left the cave this morning to hunt with

Grant." She bit the inside of her lip to keep from looking at his face. "I've searched everywhere around here. I'm going to ride the trail we took."

She finally had to meet his gaze, to see how much pain she'd brought to him. But no hint of anguish or worry or anger marked his expression. In fact, his eyes had softened.

"It is only a possession. It carries memories, yet if it is lost, we have not lost the memories. We carry them within ourselves." His voice was as steady as his gaze.

Then he nodded, as though deciding something in his mind. "Go to my mother. I will ride the trail to search for your pouch."

He turned toward his horse, but she stopped him. "You don't know where we went."

He glanced over his shoulder, turning just enough for her to catch the twinkle in his eye and the curve of his mouth. "I needed a walk this morning too."

Surprise flared through her. "You followed us?"

He turned away from her, striding toward his horse. "Stay with my mother. She will have work for you. I do not doubt this."

She waited until he swung up on his mount, then turned down the hill toward the base of the falls.

In another hour or so, the sun would begin to dip in the evening sky, and her mind drifted to the thought that hadn't gone far since Grant left. Would he reach his brother's cabin before full dark? Would Will be excited to see him? She could imagine a joyous reunion. Two brothers separated for far too many years.

When she reached the bottom of the hill, she paused before the thundering waterfall, a few drops of spray mist-ing her face. She took in a deep breath, then released it. *God, please bring Grant back to me. Let him accomplish this search that means so much to him, then bring him back to me at the ranch.*

The prayer came easier this second time. She added another. *And help White Horse find the pouch with Steps Right's necklace. Please don't let me have lost it.*

Another surge of unruly tears rose up, but she swallowed them down and started along the rocks toward the back of the falls. As she reached the ledge and stepped behind the falling water, her heart began to pound, and she couldn't shake the unnerving sensation that someone was watching her.

That couldn't be the case, unless White Horse had paused to make sure she went to his mother as he'd asked. She glanced back around the curtain of water to scan the tree line. That would be just like him. So much like an older brother that his actions teetered on the edge of overbearing at times. Especially if he thought her safety was at risk. Maybe this time it was his mother's comfort he was concerned about. Faith should have the same focus.

Turning back toward the cave, she navigated the ledge and slipped into the darkness. "It's me," she called ahead. She might wake the woman again, but alerting her presence felt like the best thing to do.

When she stepped into the dim light of the cavern, Steps Right was standing, one hand braced against the wall. "I wash." She motioned toward the water Faith had just come from.

Faith's heartbeat picked up speed, and she strode toward the woman. "Are you sure you can walk there? I'll help you." The last thing she needed was for Steps Right to injure herself more. Especially when Faith was the only one here to help.

She tucked her shoulder under Steps Right's arm on the side of her injured ankle. Together, they hobbled toward the dark corridor and the sound of the pounding waterfall.

Hopefully the woman would be able to sit and wash herself on the ledge behind the cascade. That way they wouldn't have to try to maneuver the narrow path of wet stone.

When they emerged into the light and the thundering sound of the water, Steps Right pointed to the closest part of the ledge. Faith helped her ease down to sit on the stone, then settle both feet into the water. The injured ankle was still more swollen than the other.

As she started to rise, a movement at the edge of her gaze made her jerk her focus upward, toward the path they usually walked from the bank.

Two braves stood on the ledge. Barely an arm's length away, on the other side of Steps Right. Dark paint marked their faces, making their expressions even fiercer than they might have been.

Her breath caught as panic flared through her. She might have screamed, except her throat wouldn't work. Her mind raced, scrambling to figure out who they were.

Reality slammed through her like a shove. Flies Ahead.

Except . . . neither of these men looked like those she had met. Maybe the paint disguised them. And she hadn't seen him in three years.

Did she have anything she could use as a weapon? Her pistol was in the cave. She had nothing at all. The only rocks in this area were tiny pebbles. If she threw a handful at these men, it would only anger them more. Did Steps Right have a weapon hidden in her clothing?

The man in front dropped his gaze to the older woman, whose eyes were also fixed on him. His gaze turned even harder, if that were possible, and he bit out a few sounds she couldn't decipher.

Steps Right understood them, for she responded in the same language. Her tone stayed calm, in stark contrast to his angry bark.

Faith's stomach churned as she focused on the men. Maybe she could run into the darkness of the cave and grab her gun. They would have trouble following in the thick black of the corridor. Would they hurt Steps Right while she was gone? This might be their only chance for escape.

Steps Right's words seemed to anger the men, for the one in front responded with two enraged syllables. Then he charged, lunging for Steps Right.

This time Faith did scream, even as she spun to sprint into the cave.

Something caught her dress, stopping her forward movement. Then a hand gripped her shoulder, yanking her backward. She twisted, trying to scramble away from the vise. But another arm wrapped around her middle, dragging her toward the water.

She screamed, but the sound only lasted a second as the hand on her shoulder released, only to close over her mouth like a smothering blanket. A foul stench filled her nostrils, and she could taste the grit on his skin. She couldn't breathe. Panic surged through her as she clawed at the hands, trying to escape their grip.

He was carrying her forward, along the ledge. Away from the cave.

Where was Steps Right? What was the other man doing to her?

The older woman was shorter than Faith, but likely heavier. And her bones would be far more fragile. If that other brave hoisted her like this, would he break a bone?

Faith fought harder, twisting and kicking and clawing. The arm around her waist cinched so tight, tears sprang to her eyes. If he'd grabbed any higher, he would have broken her ribs.

As he carried her around the edge of the falling water, she craned her neck to find Steps Right. She caught only a flash of movement—the other brave jerking the elderly woman up from where she sat at the water's edge.

Her ankle. Faith couldn't let anything happen to the woman who'd saved her father's life so many years ago. White Horse's mother.

She fought harder, desperation fueling every movement.

A force struck her head, slamming pain and flashes of light through her vision.

Then blackness closed in.

EIGHTEEN

As the sun dipped low in the sky, casting long shadows across the banks of the river, Grant pulled back on his reins, bringing the sweating gelding to a halt. He slipped to the ground, then led the horse to drink.

"Rest a minute, boy." He patted the animal's neck as it drank greedily.

His own belly rumbled for food, so he moved to the back of his saddle and loosened the straps of the saddlebag. As he rummaged for the pack of dried meat Faith had sent with him, his fingers finally found the rough leather of the case. He pulled it out, but this wasn't the buckskin wrapping he'd expected.

His mind scrambled for what this small, unfamiliar pouch might be. Its long cord was tied like a necklace, but it had come undone on one end. He'd definitely never seen this. Was it something of Faith's or White Horse's that had gotten mixed with his things?

He loosened the strings to open it and peered inside. Blue

crystal beads lay nestled within, and his breath caught. Was this the special necklace Faith had brought to give back to Steps Right?

He reached two fingers into the pouch to pull it out but stopped before he touched the beads. Maybe he shouldn't. If he'd somehow taken it away from her, he had to bring it back. Now.

Carefully, he gripped one of the beads and lifted it. A long string of blue crystals pulled out of the pouch, and he rested them across his hand. This was definitely the necklace. It had to be.

His clumsy fingers trembled as he lifted it back into the pouch. It would be just his luck to break the strand before he could get it back to Faith.

How in the world had it gotten in his saddle pack? She hadn't put it there on purpose, had she? No, that didn't make a bit of sense. Her entire reason to search so hard for Steps Right was to give this heirloom back to the woman. She wouldn't let it out of her possession until that was accomplished.

Once he'd pulled the pouch tightly closed, he tucked it back in the bottom of his saddlebag. The gelding had finished drinking, so he mounted again, then turned the animal back the way they'd come. "We have a delivery to make first. Then we'll find Will."

It would be close to dark by the time he made it back to the cave, though. He would have to wait until morning to start again. Disappointment pressed in his chest, but he pushed the feeling aside.

If Faith had realized she'd lost the necklace, she would be frantic. Stopping her distress was more than worth the delay. In fact, if he were honest with himself, the chance to see her again lightened his spirit.

The ride back seemed to take longer than the first time he traveled this path. But as they neared the cave, his gelding slowed even more. Grant let him ease to a walk, but the horse seemed tense. Its ears twitched, and its nostrils flared.

"Easy there, boy." He ran a soothing hand along the gelding's neck. But even as he sought to calm his mount, apprehension settled like a shroud over his own shoulders.

Dusk had fallen heavily, and the familiar landscape now felt fraught with shadows. In twenty strides, he would ride out of the woods and see the waterfall in the distance. He could already hear the murmur of its thunder. Maybe that's what made his horse uneasy.

Something shifted among the trees ahead, near the edge of the forest. He tensed, reaching for the rifle tucked in its scabbard. He should have had it across his lap. But as he was pulling the weapon out, a figure appeared in the evening light.

He lifted the barrel just as recognition slipped in. White Horse.

Grant breathed out, his heart thundering far too fast as he lowered the gun to rest across his legs.

White Horse raised a finger to his lips and strode toward Grant. The worry crept back into his gut, but he kept silent as he nudged his gelding faster. When they reached him, Grant slipped to the ground to face the other man.

"My mother and Faith are gone." White Horse spoke quietly, but his words struck Grant like he'd shouted.

"Gone? Where? How?" Steps Right had barely walked

since they first found her. How could she and Faith leave? And why would White Horse allow it?

Why would Faith leave while Grant was gone? Hadn't she told him to come back here? To bring his brother? That long ago pain crashed in, bringing a deluge of darkness.

Just like the Flagstones. Promising to be there, then gone.

"Taken." White Horse spoke again, and Grant forced himself to pull from that dark place to focus on the words.

Taken? What did he mean? He studied White Horse's expression for a hint. The worry there was impossible to miss.

Taken. Faith and Steps Right?

The reality jolted him fully out of the heavy cloud, back to clearer thinking. "Who did it? The man Steps Right was hiding from?"

"Only a few tracks, but I think Flies Ahead and another." White Horse scanned their surroundings. "They rode into river. I look for more sign."

Anger surged through him as his mind raced, conjuring images of Faith in danger, her blue eyes wide with fear.

"How did they get close?" He didn't want to cast guilt on the man, not when he'd already shown he would go to great lengths to protect both women.

White Horse met his gaze. "Faith could not find the pouch she wore around her neck. I went to search the place she thought she lost it."

Grant's chest tightened. "Did it hold the blue bead necklace? I found it in my saddlebag. That's why I came back. I don't know how it got there, but I knew she'd worry." How could such a simple mishap lead to something so awful?

See, God? This is exactly why I can't trust you. How could you let this happen?

White Horse was already moving past him, toward the river. "I search for tracks."

Grant called quietly after him, "Should I look on the other side of the river?" That way they could move faster and be more certain they weren't missing a vital clue.

"Get my horse first. Then come to me."

"All right." Grant turned back to his gelding and swung into the saddle.

God, this would be a good time to make up for letting us all down. Help us find Faith and Steps Right. Don't let Flies Ahead hurt them.

Faith moaned against the pounding in her head as she fought to pull from sleep. The side of her scalp burned, and she reached up to feel the spot. Her fingers touched something wet, and the contact made the ache splitting her skull hammer even harder.

She groaned again, trying to push through the pain and open her eyes. When she finally succeeded, the world swam before her. Dark, but with a bright light blinding her. She blinked several times to clear her vision.

This darkness was the dim light of night, and the brightness came from a campfire. Her arms ached, and she tried to shift them to a more comfortable position. They wouldn't move. That's when her cloudy mind finally came alive.

She was tied.

She sat upright against a narrow tree, her hands bound behind it. The rough bark pressed against her back, and a root poked her bottom.

As her vision cleared, she caught sight of a figure nearby.

Steps Right sat against another tree, a little more than an arm's length away. Her head rested to the side, the light from the campfire shining on her closed eyes.

Faith's heart picked up speed. She wasn't dead, was she?

As Faith strained for signs of movement, she finally caught the slow raising and lowering of her shoulders as she breathed. Asleep, then. Or maybe unconscious, as Faith had been.

Her chest tightened, and she turned her focus to the shadows around the campfire. Two men sat at the edge of its light. One was the brave who'd spoken to Steps Right back at the mouth of the cave, then attacked her.

Just beyond him sat Flies Ahead. His face was marked with black paint like the other man, but he was too familiar not to recognize. Maybe it was the expanse of his shoulders and the way he held himself like he was in charge.

He would be chief one day, after all. Or maybe he already was. Had his grandfather died in the three years since she and her sisters had gone to their village looking for Steps Right?

She flicked her gaze around the area once more to look for the other man, the one who'd grabbed her. No sign of him. Maybe he was standing guard in the shadows or had been sent on an errand.

White Horse. Her stomach clutched. Had they gone back to find him? Maybe Flies Ahead had more men, a group strong enough to overpower White Horse.

She pulled harder at her wrists, testing the strength of the cord that bound them. What did White Horse think when he came back and found her and his mother missing?

Did he recognize signs of the struggle? He was an excellent tracker, so hopefully he'd find prints from the men.

She struggled to remember what had happened after the brave grabbed her. She'd fought him as he carried her along the ledge. She'd seen that quick glimpse of the other man grabbing Steps Right. Then her captor had started carrying her over the boulders toward the grass. She couldn't grasp any memories after that. Maybe that was when he'd knocked her unconscious.

The reminder made the ache at the side of her head spring alive again. Maybe he'd knocked her against the rock wall to stop her fighting.

She looked to Steps Right again. Had they done the same to her? Faith's belly roiled. A woman of her age, already injured . . . how badly had they hurt her?

Steps Right's face didn't look in pain, only lifeless as she slept. *God, please let her wake soon.* Maybe she would know how to get out of this. Perhaps she could bargain with Flies Ahead.

The men by the fire were speaking softly in their own language, so Faith couldn't understand. But she studied them, trying to make out any clues from their body language and tone. They seemed relaxed, as if they had all the time in the world.

Steps Right shifted, drawing Faith's focus back to her. Her eyes were open, though her head still rested at an angle. Her gaze met Faith's, but it was impossible to tell what she was thinking or feeling. Maybe she was trying to make sense of what was happening, as Faith had when she first woke up.

Slowly, Steps Right lifted her head, easing her shoulders

so she could see the men without straining. Could she hear them well enough to understand their words? Probably.

Waiting was hard as she allowed Steps Right time to listen and think. But what else could they do? Speaking to each other would bring Flies Ahead's attention on them, which couldn't be good.

Surely White Horse was coming. She just had to make sure the men didn't hurt Steps Right until then.

NINETEEN

Grant stared at the ground beside the river, searching for any clues in the early morning light that might reveal the path taken by Flies Ahead and his men. The gentle rustle of flowing water belied the urgency in his heart.

He and White Horse had hunted for several hours in the night, moving impossibly slow so they didn't miss anything in the near-moonless night. He'd slept little, lying on a single blanket and straining for any sound, doing his best not to wonder where Faith was every moment. Was she frightened? Hurt? Did she have a comfortable place to sleep? Most likely not.

"Here."

He honed his focus to where White Horse pointed to a patch of ground near the water's edge. "See how dirt is loose? They cover tracks."

Grant crouched, running his fingers over the subtle indentions in the muddy soil. Then he lifted his gaze to search for the next steps.

At first, he could see nothing similar to this brushed ground. But . . . were those leaves turned with the darker sides up? It was hard to tell in the dim light, especially since a night had passed, bringing with it the dampness of morning.

White Horse had moved ahead, and now pointed to another place where the edge of a hoofprint was barely discernible. Grant straightened and stepped quicker to catch up with him as they led their horses. The trail was so faint, he couldn't be certain this truly was the way Flies Ahead had gone.

But White Horse seemed sure. Or at least he didn't voice his questions aloud.

God, let him be right. Show us the way. Maybe he was a hypocrite for pleading for help when he'd blamed God for this whole disaster just last night.

But if there was a chance God would help them, the Almighty who created the earth knew where Faith and Steps Right were right now. *Help us reach them in time to stop any harm.* He hadn't been able to bring himself to ask White Horse what the warriors would do to the women.

But he needed to know where the man suspected Flies Ahead would be taking them. When White Horse motioned to another patch of brushed ground, Grant took the chance to ask him. "They spent time covering their tracks. Where do you think they're going?"

White Horse lifted his gaze to the mountains not far ahead of them. So far, they'd had to maneuver rocky terrain since the river. But soon the terrain would turn to boulder-strewn slopes. How much harder would it be to find Flies Ahead's tracks then?

"He may wish to take my mother back to the village. To make her stand before the council so her punishment can be changed." His jaw hardened. "She has already done this once. They made her leave her home and the people who are her family. But this not enough for the son with vengeance in his heart."

Flies Ahead was bent on retribution for the death of his father. If he killed White Horse's mother, would White Horse then set out on that same quest? When would the bloodshed end?

The oppressive weight of it all sank over him. Such a vendetta might not end until it took every last person dear to both families.

Unless someone chose to forgive.

White Horse had continued on, pointing to each track as he passed it, which left Grant mired in this painful question. If any man had the strength and integrity to forgive such an atrocity, White Horse just might be able. But would he be willing?

If an enemy hunted down and killed Will—Grant's last blood relative—would he be able to let it go without retaliation? Probably not. And Faith . . . He'd been trying not to let his mind consider her. But if they found both women dead . . .

Fury surged through him, lengthening his stride and making his breath come hard.

He clenched his jaw. Little by little, she'd seeped into his life. So much that the thought of her not being there in his future . . . A life like that looked far too dark to contemplate.

Faith had become light and hope in his life. She'd taught

him what it meant to be strong, to fulfill a promise no matter what the risk. And she'd done it all with a smile that radiated warmth to his deepest core.

No matter what, he couldn't let Flies Ahead snuff out that light. He couldn't—he wouldn't—let Faith down.

But even with that determination, he had a feeling it might take a Power greater than what he and White Horse both possessed to rescue the women unharmed.

❧

Faith studied the three braves across the camp, straining to make out anything in their Peigan tongue. Flies Ahead stood tall in front of the other two, his back to Faith, fists clenched at his sides. Though their voices were loud and heated, they spoke too quickly for her to pick out any of the words White Horse had taught her.

She glanced over at Steps Right, who sat quietly, head resting against the tree she was tied to. She must be as uncomfortable as Faith. More so, for she had the swollen ankle that must pain her.

But the older woman's face was a calm mask, betraying little emotion as she listened to the exchange. Only the subtle tightness around her eyes and the slight downturn of her mouth hinted at concern.

"*Misstapok'a!*" Flies Ahead spat, the command cutting through the air. His men fell silent, watching him as though waiting for his next command. "*Nitakit!*" Flies Ahead flapped his hand in a shooing motion, and one of the men— the one who'd attacked her and had been gone all night— turned and sprinted into the trees.

Faith's pulse quickened as Flies Ahead turned toward

them, his cold gaze locking on Steps Right first, then flicking to her. He started toward them, and she fought to keep her shiver from showing. She couldn't let him know how afraid she was.

When the third man showed up that morning, she'd half expected them to pack up camp and hoist her and Steps Right back on the horses with them. Since they'd not been killed yet, surely Flies Ahead planned to take them back to his village.

But they still sat here, tied to these trees. What else could he be waiting for? More men to return from errands he'd sent them on?

Flies Ahead stopped three strides from them, the perfect position to look down on her and Steps Right without shifting his gaze.

The perfect position for her to see the hatred darkening his eyes.

He snarled, spitting out his words. "White Horse not save you."

Though Steps Right didn't make a sound, Faith could feel her tension even without looking at her. She didn't dare take her focus off the fierce warrior.

"Hear now." Flies Ahead's tone dropped to an icy pitch. "I kill." He pointed from Steps Right to Faith. "Slow. Much hurt." Then his gaze locked on Steps Right again. "Your son and white man watch."

White man? Faith's entire body froze, her lungs refusing to draw breath. Grant? Had he returned with Will already? That seemed unlikely. He would have found his brother after dark last night. But since Will knew Steps Right, maybe he'd agreed to set out first thing this morning. Still, it didn't seem possible Grant could have brought his brother back so quickly.

Oh, God, help us get out of this mess without anyone getting hurt. Not White Horse or Grant. And definitely not Steps Right.

Flies Ahead glared at her, as though he'd listened to her thoughts, or maybe he saw the confusion on her face. "Punish white man for taking hunt from Flies Ahead's gun."

Taking hunt from Flies Ahead's gun? Her head ached too much to decipher his meaning, especially with the broken English. Then a memory slipped in. Back when she and Grant had still been traveling with Parson's group, she had helped Grant smoke a side of elk meat. He'd said he found the animal already killed. That the hunter had abandoned the kill. Or maybe the elk hadn't died right away but wandered a while and the shooter hadn't been able to find it.

She cleared her throat. "You shot the bull elk? Grant waited for the hunter to come."

Hatred darkened the man's gaze. "No man takes from Flies Ahead." He flicked a gaze over his shoulder, then turned back to her. "Three times I send man to punish him. Now I make suffer."

She stared at him. "You attacked Grant before? You followed us?"

He jerked his head toward the other man. "Crooked Knife. He run. Bring dishonor on his father's lodge."

All the times strange things had happened . . . those had been Flies Ahead's doing?

He raised his chin, the act making him look even more like a chief than before. "We go to rendezvous for trade. White man steal elk. Follow to make pay." A light flickered in his eyes. "We see son of Steps Right. The gods smile on

Flies Ahead. Lead us to the one who kills the father of Flies Ahead."

He turned his focus to Steps Right, then spat on the ground at her feet. "Your son watch you suffer as I watch my father. He see your body when spirit no more." His jaw flexed. "Then I kill him. I will bring honor on the lodge of my father once more."

He spat again, this time on the hem of Steps Right's dress.

Faith had to work to keep from venting her anger on the man. How dare he insult a woman, especially an elder, in such a way? But she made herself sit still. Any movement, any fight against her ropes or his goading would only please him.

He wouldn't win. She couldn't let him.

Finally, the man turned and strode to the far corner of the camp to stare through the pine trunks at the valley below. Watching for White Horse and Grant, no doubt.

She slid a look at Steps Right. They still hadn't dared to speak to each other, but she needed to know if Steps Right was injured more than before. If at all possible, she had to find a way of escape before White Horse and Grant arrived. Maybe now, while there were only two men and they weren't fully focused on her and Steps Right.

She kept her voice in her quietest whisper. "Can you walk?"

Steps Right didn't look at her, just let her unfocused gaze wander beyond the camp. But she gave a tiny dip of her chin.

Good.

Now she had to figure out how to get them untied.

Did they have anything sharp? She certainly didn't. If

Steps Right possessed such a tool, she would have already used it, or at least mentioned she had something.

The tree Faith was tied to had smooth bark, so it might take a day to scrape through her binding by rubbing the cord against the trunk. She would be willing to try it, though.

She slid her wrists up and down behind her. Pain shot through her upper arms at the awkward angle. Worse than that, she had to lean forward with each movement, making her actions far too obvious. Moving her wrists side to side was nearly as bad.

If she could get near fire, she could burn the rope. But that was impossible with her hands tied behind the tree.

She would have to find a person to set them free. She glanced at the second brave, Crooked Knife, the one who'd first spoken to them behind the waterfall. He hadn't come over to them but once, when he brought a cup of water for them each to take a sip from.

He was a little shorter than Flies Ahead but had thicker shoulders. That was probably how he'd managed to carry Steps Right's heavier body. Hopefully he *had* carried her, not made her walk on her bad ankle. How much worse had the struggle injured her?

If she helped him understand how injured Steps Right was, would he take pity on them and help them escape? Not likely. Especially since he was the one who took them captive in the first place. At Flies Ahead's orders, of course. They would find no ally in either man.

Could Flies Ahead be reasoned with? Did he possess a scrap of mercy? Maybe if she helped him see how killing them in cold blood would be so much worse than his father dying of an illness.

A look at the man's hard profile—jaw set and fists clenched at his sides as he stood watch—made it seem so unlikely.

God, what can I do? She'd been praying all day, but she couldn't tell if the Lord heard her. *Please, show me what to do.*

Not you but Me.

The idea slipped in so quietly, yet it staked a solid claim in her mind. *Is that you, Lord?* For so long, she'd wanted a real answer from God when she prayed. Something that she could see or feel and know for certain was Him communicating.

She'd never expected His voice to come as such a quiet thought. How many times before had He answered her in this way but she'd missed it?

Not you but Me.

So she shouldn't try for an escape? She should just sit here, tied to this tree in the hot sun, and wait? Thirst was already making her head ache, even more than the low pounding from her injury.

She slid a glance at Steps Right. It was one thing to risk her own life on whether these quiet words were from God, and if they were, whether He would actually carry out the answer He promised.

Steps Right must have felt her gaze, for she turned her head just enough for their gazes to meet. Her aged voice quavered in a half whisper as she spoke. "Pray. We pray."

It sounded like Steps Right was willing to wait on God for deliverance too. Faith dipped a nod. Interesting that the woman would say those words—the only thing she'd spoken since their capture—at that very moment Faith had been questioning God.

How many other times in her life had she received direction from God, and simply hadn't recognized it? And then she'd blamed Him in her heart for not answering—every time.

Guilt pressed through her, and she squeezed her eyes shut against it. *I'm sorry, Lord. Forgive me for being headstrong and untrusting. I'm leaving this to you now, as you said. I pray my obedience hasn't come too late.*

TWENTY

G rant wanted to shout his frustration as he stared at the ground in front of them. He didn't yell, of course, only allowed himself a low growl. How could the tracks simply fade away?

He and White Horse had been searching for hours today, in addition to what they'd been able to accomplish last night before darkness fell. They'd had to move ridiculously slow with every step, since the men had taken such care to conceal signs of their passing.

The prints had disappeared several times along the way, but White Horse always picked them up a little farther ahead. The two who'd taken Faith and Steps Right hadn't kept a perfectly straight path—few could with all these trees—but they'd kept moving in the same general direction.

Just before they lost the trail, the route had seemed to curve a little. Was it because the captors were preparing to circle back to their camp, somewhere much closer to the waterfall? Or had they simply been riding with the lay of the land?

This time, though, no matter how much farther he and White Horse rode, they couldn't find the tracks again.

"There is a ridge ahead." White Horse pointed to the left where a rocky spire rose slightly higher than the trees. "Maybe we see from above."

That might be their best option. Grant sighed and nudged his gelding forward. "Let's try it."

As they rode up the hill, the horse's hooves clattered on loose rocks. The slope steepened, with boulders perched too close together for their animals to pass, so he and White Horse dismounted and climbed higher on foot. At the top of the ridge, Grant stood beside White Horse as they both stared out over the terrain.

Treetops spread out before them, a mass of lodgepole pine branches covering the gentle slope down. The green stopped as the land flattened into a wide valley. That might be a stream winding through the middle. Beyond the grassland rose a mountain with trees dotting its base. The cliffs climbed steeply into a peak far higher than the one on which they stood.

He shifted his focus back to the trees in front of them, searching for any sign of movement or presence of a person. He strained, tracking his gaze out over the valley, then scanned as far as he could up the far slope.

"Look." White Horse pointed to a place just below their vantage point. Through the branches, a spot of brown moved.

Grant held his breath as he focused on the motion, working to make out shapes. That looked like the brown of a horse, but . . . where was the rider?

The animal below shifted, revealing a flash of tan at one

end. A set of . . . antlers? Near the animal, another spot of brown appeared.

Grant's heart sank. "I think they're deer. Two of them. Maybe more."

White Horse nodded, and Grant started his visual search over again, this time moving from his left all the way to his far right. He'd just about scanned the entire area when White Horse straightened beside him. He must be ready to go back for the horses and search again.

But instead he turned to Grant. "We need to pray."

Those weren't at all the words he'd expected.

White Horse closed his eyes without hesitation. Was he going to pray aloud? Should Grant bow his head too? Headmaster Lawton had always required it as a sign of respect.

A tiny part of him wondered if White Horse would be praying to the same God the headmaster had. They were such different men. And didn't the Natives worship things like the sun and moon? Even though White Horse had learned to pray to God Almighty, he might still cling to his old religion too.

White Horse spoke in a voice that held quiet strength. "Creator God. Our Father. Give us vision. Protect this sister. Protect my mother. Take us to them. I pray through Jesus, the Son who did no bad thing."

The words were different from the long-winded petitions Headmaster Lawton had spoken, but every bit as earnest.

Grant desperately wanted these same things White Horse had asked, so he added his own "Amen."

White Horse lifted his head and met Grant's gaze. "The great God knows where they are. We ask Him to show us. We ask Him to fight this battle for us and bring victory."

He held Grant's focus for a long minute—a minute in which he seemed to be trying to infuse his solid faith into Grant.

Part of him wished that could happen. That he could find the certainty this man possessed that God would answer. That the Almighty would make the way plain and bring them success. *God, how do I find that?*

There was no answer. He shouldn't have expected a voice to boom from heaven.

But still, an ache rose up in his throat. *God, if you're up there. Keep Faith and Steps Right safe. Help us find them. Let them know we're coming.*

Helplessness hung heavy around him like a smothering blanket. What more could they do?

"The great God knows where they are. We ask Him to show us."

White Horse's words slipped back through his mind. *Show us then, God. Take us to them.* His eyes burned, and he no longer had the strength to hold back the tears. *If you're real, take me to Faith right now.*

Don't come, Grant. Please, don't come.

It was hard to tell how much of Faith's clenched belly came from sitting all day in the August sun with no food and little water, or whether her middle had twisted into a knot from hours of watching Flies Ahead and Crooked Knife sit at their lookout perches. Each man kept guard with his rifle across his lap, hands positioned on the weapon so they could easily lift and aim whenever Grant and White Horse approached.

Flies Ahead had said he wanted the men to watch while he tortured and killed her and Steps Right. But had he changed his mind and decided to punish the two of them by making them watch Grant and White Horse die? She wouldn't be able to bear it.

Don't come, Grant. Both of you, stay away. Maybe Flies Ahead would reveal when they were approaching and she could call out to warn them.

She was so weary, her eyelids begged to let her fade to oblivion. But she made herself keep steadily breathing, doing her best to stay alert for any opportunity to warn the men.

She'd made peace with that fact that she would probably die soon. Made peace with the God who saw her, even in this remote mountain country. She was a tiny dot too small to show on a map of this massive mountain wilderness, but God saw her and had a good plan for her.

Even now, she could feel the peace of His presence. The warmth of the Father's arms wrapped around her. She would be content if she were taken from this world to be forever with Him.

But Grant . . .

I don't think he knows you, Lord. Don't let these men kill him. He needs time. Needs someone to show him the truth about you.

If only she'd done that when she had the chance. Grant had encouraged her faith more than she'd nurtured his. What had he said? *"What your sisters have is real. It can be real for you too. I don't know how to find it, but I think if your heart is open . . . if you ask Him, God will be there. He'll answer you. Every time. It might not be in ways you expect, but it will be Him answering."*

How could he say those things if God's love wasn't real for him? Yet she'd gotten the feeling Grant thought God was for others, not for himself. Maybe he thought the Almighty looked past him. *Show him the truth, Lord. Don't let him be lost.*

A shuffling sounded from somewhere through the trees, and she forced her eyes to focus. Both men jumped to their feet, and Flies Ahead raised his rifle against his shoulder. But he didn't squint down the barrel to aim, just kept watching the trees beyond their camp.

Grant and White Horse must be approaching. If it was the other man who'd come with Flies Ahead, they wouldn't be aiming guns at him.

She needed to warn them somehow. She strained against her bindings as she scanned the supplies littering the camp. Even if there was something she could use as a weapon or to signal Grant and White Horse, she couldn't get free to reach it.

Flies Ahead shifted, then began to back away from his position, moving into the camp. He still kept his rifle against his shoulder, even raising it more so he'd be able to aim easily.

Crooked Knife looked over at him, a question in his gaze. She couldn't see Flies Ahead's expression well, but he must have signaled for Crooked Knife to move back with them. What were they planning?

The answer came clear within seconds as the men came to stand on either side of her and Steps Right. Crooked Knife halted on Faith's left, and Flies Ahead positioned himself on the other side of the older woman.

Both kept their guns pointed at the source of the rustling sounds.

Her throat tightened so much she couldn't swallow or

breathe. Whoever approached would see the two braves first. Would they be able to react quickly enough once they realized they were walking into an ambush?

She would have to alert them.

Sounds had begun to drift through the trees beyond the camp. Horses snorting and saddles squeaking. They were close enough they would hear a yell. She had to act.

She sucked in a breath and shouted, "Don't come farther! It's a trap!"

Flies Ahead whipped around, leaping in front of Steps Right to aim his gun at Faith. "Quiet!"

At least that protected Steps Right a little, drawing the weapon away from her. Crooked Knife had also pointed his rifle at Faith. She'd never felt so vulnerable, strapped to this tree with two powerful guns pointed at her.

She was going to die, but she wouldn't let anyone else come with her, if she could help it. Not until she knew they were ready to meet the Lord.

She screamed again, "Get away, Grant. It's a trap! Turn and run." At least her yelling was distracting Flies Ahead from whatever attack he'd planned for the men.

Flies Ahead pressed the rifle barrel against her temple. As cold steel pressed hard into her skin, out of the corner of her eye, she caught sight of a person breaking through the trees.

But the hard push of metal that bent her neck forced her focus fully on the man nearest her. She had to look from the side of her gaze to see his face, his eyes wild now instead of the cold calculation of before. Was it better or worse that he seemed to have lost his self-control?

She wasn't afraid of him. Nor of death.

She sucked in a small breath. "Run, Grant! Get away from here. Go!" She knew it was him. Every part of her could feel his presence. White Horse was likely there too, but Grant led the charge into camp.

She couldn't look at what they were doing. Couldn't take her eyes off this madman who might well end her life with his next breath.

"Drop the gun." Grant's voice called across the open space, cold and hard with fury.

Flies Ahead's eyes flared wide in a vicious glare. "No."

Yea, though I walk through the valley of the shadow of death, I will fear no evil: for thou art with me.

The verse she'd memorized as a child wrapped around her like a hedge of protection from the man. *Father, be with me. I will fear no evil for you are with me.*

Flies Ahead's grin faltered. Maybe because she didn't show the terror he'd hoped for?

"Drop rifle or I kill." He snarled the words, flicking his gaze between her and the two men she could just see at the corner of her vision. A tremble quivered through him. She might not have felt it except for the steel-encased explosive connecting her head to his hands.

She scrambled for another verse in the recesses of her mind. *For he shall give his angels charge over thee, to keep thee in all thy ways.*

Keep me from fear, Father. Give me peace in you.

"Sit. Or I shoot her." Flies Ahead's voice rose higher than before.

She wanted to squeeze her eyes closed so she didn't have to watch this man in her last moments. But she couldn't sit by and let this killer hurt anyone else.

Summoning a final scrap of courage, she made her voice as level and strong as she could manage with the steel barrel still pressed hard against her temple. "Don't do anything he says."

Even as she spoke the words, she knew Grant wouldn't obey them. He would try to save her. "I mean it, Grant." She had to speak through clenched teeth so she didn't shift her head and make Flies Ahead accidentally pull the trigger. "This isn't worth it. Leave and stay away from him. For me. Please."

If she went this way, she at least wanted to die knowing she'd saved his and White Horse's lives. Steps Right too.

But no . . . really she wanted to die knowing she'd helped save them all eternally. *Yes, Lord.* White Horse and Steps Right already knew the true God. But Grant . . .

Talking was easier now that she'd begun, so she continued in that strong voice, though she kept her gaze on Flies Ahead. "Grant, you were right when you said that if I asked God for help, He would be there. He's with me now, giving me strength."

She breathed in a bit of that strength and continued. "But what you need to know is that He loves you too. More than you can possibly imagine. You don't have to do anything to be worthy of it. He already thinks you're worth *everything*. Worth His love. Worth His son dying so He could show you exactly how much He loves you. You only have to open yourself enough to receive that love. He won't take it away either. Not like everything else you've lost."

Including me. The thought nearly made a sob slip out. If he felt half as much for her as she did him, watching her die would be one more hard blow. She had to do everything she could to ease the strength of it. To give him hope.

She sucked in enough breath to keep talking. "There's something else you need to know, Grant." Her voice quavered, but she had to get these words out. "I love you. I have for weeks now. I think ever since you kept my secret with the trappers. You're a good man, Grant Allen. The best of men. I made peace with God, just like you said to. I'll be going to heaven. I want more than anything to see you there."

Grant spoke then, his words not aimed at her, his voice hard and unyielding. "Get away from her. Both of you." His footsteps scuffed the ground as he walked toward them.

Faith couldn't breathe. She didn't want this to happen. Didn't want to be saved at Grant's expense. At anyone's expense.

Yet maybe once Flies Ahead took the rifle away, she could do something to stop his revenge for good.

As Grant came within arm's reach, he extended a hand for the rifle.

Flies Ahead snarled at him. "Do not come closer."

She had to do something. Her hands were tied, but not her feet. With Flies Ahead looking at Grant, she might be quick enough to stop him. She wouldn't be able to take out the other brave too, but maybe this would distract him just long enough.

Without letting it show on the outside, she took in a deep breath, tensed her legs, then thrust her boots out at Flies Ahead's kneecaps with every bit of force she could muster. As he stumbled backward, she kicked one foot upward into the softer part of his middle.

His grunt sounded just before his rifle exploded.

Gunpowder clouded the air as the blast reverberated through the camp and the valley beyond.

Then a scream of pain overwhelmed the echo of the report.

Who'd been shot? *God, let them live. Please let them live.*

Something flew at her from her right, striking a blow that clanged through her head. Too much like the pain from when she first woke up tied to this tree.

Movement swarmed around her. But the pain and flashes of light that consumed her focus couldn't keep up with it all.

Grant's shout sounded through the pain ricocheting through her skull. But she couldn't make out the words.

Was that another scream of pain?

Or maybe the blast of a rifle.

She couldn't stand the ringing.

Her mind couldn't contain the chaos and agony.

She tried to press her hands to her head, but she was falling.

She squeezed her eyes shut.

Another blow slammed into the back of her head.

Then it all faded to black.

TWENTY-ONE

G rant stroked the hair from Faith's brow as he studied her beautiful pale face. *God, please don't take her. Don't take her from me.*

So much had happened during that fight. The bullet from Flies Ahead's gun had struck the other brave in the belly. He lay on the ground now, a blanket covering his lifeless body and the pool of blood around him. He'd bled out almost before they secured Flies Ahead and turned to help him.

Then a third brave had appeared. White Horse had caught sight of him in just enough time to duck the flying tomahawk. Grant's rifle had convinced the man to give in easily after that, and now both he and Flies Ahead sat tied to trees nearby.

Faith lost consciousness during the struggle too. He still had no idea whether something struck her in the head or if she fainted from the strain. The latter didn't seem likely. Not with the strength Faith possessed.

He glanced over her body to Steps Right, who sat on Faith's other side. She seemed to have weathered the kidnapping as well as could be expected. The lines around her eyes had deepened, probably from exhaustion. She'd assured them she was well, and that nothing more could be done for Faith until she awoke.

Behind his mother, White Horse stood guard, rifle aimed at the two sullen men bound nearby. Steps Right had said she'd only seen the three men, but White Horse looked fierce enough to take on the attack of a hundred more if they swarmed into camp. Grant could well imagine the mixture of relief and anger the man must feel, seeing how his mother had been treated here.

He turned back to Faith. Steps Right said neither of them had been hurt by the braves, other than being knocked unconscious when they were kidnapped.

Was that why a second blow had laid Faith low for so long? It had been at least a half hour since the attack.

Her chest rose and fell with a steady rhythm, but her tanned skin had turned so pale. Her face that usually showed such expression lay still.

"Faith." His throat rasped, so he cleared it. "Wake up." The rasp was gone, but he couldn't keep his voice from cracking. "Please."

She'd said she loved him. More than anything, he wanted the chance to tell her the same. To take her in his arms and hold her. To never let her go.

She'd said he made her better. How on earth that could be true, he didn't know. But he was tired of pushing her away. If she wanted to love him, he would give her everything he had. All the time and attention and everything he owned. He would protect her as best he could. No matter what it took.

And he would treasure her. The way she deserved to be treasured.

"He loves you too. More than you can possibly imagine. You don't have to do anything to be worthy of it."

Faith's words threaded through his mind. They couldn't really be true, though. Faith loved him because she was just that wonderful.

But God couldn't love him. *Didn't* love him. He'd already proven that when He didn't answer Grant's prayers.

He already thinks you're worth everything.

She'd put such emphasis on that last word. As though God would give up everything He had. His power. The entire world He'd created, for Grant.

"Worth His love. Worth His son dying so He could show you exactly how much He loves you. You only have to open yourself enough to receive that love."

A burn crept back into his throat, searing him. He swallowed. If only that were true. If only God did care about him even a tiny portion of what Faith had said.

"You only have to open yourself enough to receive that love."

He lifted his head to look up at the sky above. *How do I do that? How do I open myself to you?*

He sat there for a long moment. Waiting. Would there be a voice that spoke aloud? A knowing in his mind?

He waited. Listening. There was nothing audible. Nothing that spoke clearly in his mind. But deep inside him, there was . . . an easing. Like some of his tension relaxed.

Maybe this was what Faith had meant. He lifted a silent prayer to the heavens. *I want to open myself to you. If you're willing to love me, I want it. I'll do what you ask. I'll make myself worthy.*

Again, Faith's words slipped in. *"You don't have to do anything to be worthy of it."* That's what she'd said, but this time he didn't hear her voice in his mind. It was more like a knowing, down in his chest. In his spirit.

He squeezed his eyes closed as emotion welled through him. *Is that you, God? Can you really take me the way I am? I want it. I want what you'll give. Your love, if you'll offer it to a man like me.*

The emotion overwhelmed his mind, and he kept his eyes squeezed shut. Absorbing it all. Soaking in this . . . this peace. There were no words, but it was more than he'd ever felt.

She'd never seen such joy on Grant's face.

As Faith watched him now, with his eyes closed tight and his expression nearly glowing with peace and pleasure, she could only think of one thing that might have placed it there.

And she wouldn't interrupt this moment with the Lord for anything.

Thank you, Father.

After a while, he opened his eyes. Then blinked. She squeezed his hand, the one she'd been holding when she awoke.

He blinked again as he jerked his gaze down to her. His eyes widened, like he was still trying to come back to the present. "Faith?"

She smiled, though her lips were so dry, they cracked with the movement. "Grant."

He pushed into action, leaning over her, a mixture of worry and wonder taking over his expression. He still held her hand, but with his other, he stroked her hair. "Are you hurt? What happened?"

It took too much energy to remember, so she didn't try. Her head pounded, and she was so thirsty. "Water."

"Here." Steps Right's voice came from her other side.

Grant reached to take a tin cup from the older woman, then focused on Faith. "Can you sit up a little?"

She squinted against the pain, and with his hand behind her head to help, she lifted enough to drink. The first sip ached—in the best way possible. Her throat burned as the water seeped through the parched places.

She paused to breathe before taking another. This swallow didn't hurt as much as it soothed. She gulped down a third sip, then a fourth.

The water was clearing her head, so she leaned on her elbow and took the cup from Grant. When she finished the last bit, she handed him the cup and eased back to the ground to take stock of things.

She could remember being tied to a tree. . . .

Steps Right. She turned quickly to find the woman, but the sudden movement sent flashes of light and pain through her skull. She squeezed her eyes shut and pressed a hand to her face. But she had to know if the older woman was hurt. "Steps Right?" Her voice came out a mumble, but it must have been loud enough.

A hand rested on her shoulder. "I am here. Rest. Eat."

Her belly didn't feel like it could handle food, but Grant's voice rumbled from her other side. "You probably need a good broth, but that will take a while to make. Pemmican will help for now."

Maybe she could manage a little. Especially if it would ease the worry in his voice.

He pressed a piece into her hand, and she put it in her

mouth to chew. The taste did seem to ease the unrest in her middle. She opened her eyes and focused on chewing. Once she swallowed, he fed her another. After she'd downed three bites, her head finally shifted from pounding to a quieter ache, and she could think more clearly.

She turned her gaze to Grant and let her own eyes roam his face. Taking in every handsome feature. Every strong line. Every mark she loved. He wore several days' scruff. Enough that some might call it a beard.

He looked wonderful. So much her heart welled so full it ached.

"You had me worried."

She lifted her focus to his eyes, sinking deep in their earnest depths.

It still seemed too wonderful that he was here. The last she'd seen him, he was riding away to find his brother. But something had changed that. She swallowed to clear her throat. "Did you find Will?"

He shook his head. "After I'd ridden about an hour, I discovered your pouch with the necklace in my saddlebag. I knew you would be frantic when you realized you lost it, so I turned around and rode back to the waterfall. Before I got there, White Horse found me and told me you both were missing." His gaze flicked up to Steps Right, then he refocused on her. "I don't think I've ever been so worried in my life."

She reached for Grant's hand, and he wove his fingers between hers. "God brought us through." She smiled at him, something she could do much easier now with a bit of strength returned.

Grant lifted her hand to his mouth and pressed a kiss to

the backs of her fingers, then held them against his chest. "I know. I . . . still can't believe it."

She searched his eyes. "Did you hear what I said? When he had the gun on me?" That part she could remember well. That desperate need to tell Grant the most important things.

His eyes sparked, maybe at the memory of the danger. "You mean when my heart nearly stopped? I can't believe you took such risks. He would have killed you."

Then his gaze turned earnest again. So intense it made her lightheaded. "I heard every word. It nearly undid me." He lifted her fingers to kiss them again, then curled them back against his chest. "I did what you said. I opened myself to God. I didn't think He cared. But He showed me."

Even through her exhaustion, joy welled through her. Tears blurred her vision, and one or two slipped out before she could wipe them away. "Grant." She sniffed, blinking so she could see him clearly.

He leaned forward to brush his thumb across her cheek, maybe clearing away another drop. "And as for that other, I don't think it's fair that you got to tell me you love me first." A touch of sadness tinged his gaze. "But I suppose that's what I needed to kick me forward."

He gathered her other hand so he was holding them both against his chest. She relished the feel of his cotton shirt. The warmth of his body, whole and uninjured. The way he was looking at her as though she mattered more to him than anything else in the world.

"I love you too, Faith Collins. I don't have words for how much." His voice cracked in a way that threatened to bring on the tears again. "I still don't know how I came to be lucky enough to have your love." He paused. "Or God's."

She stroked a thumb across the back of his hand. Just a little nudge of encouragement.

"But I'm thankful for you both. I almost lost you today, and it made me realize how thickheaded I was being." He paused to study her. Maybe he was waiting for her to answer, but the hope inside her was too strong for her to speak.

"I don't want to be separated from you again. I know I need to ask for your hand officially." His brows lowered. "To your sisters. And maybe White Horse too."

She smiled and nodded—just a little, for the movement made her head pound. "Probably all of them."

He dipped his chin. "All of them, then. But until I can, I'm staking my claim here and now."

He shifted so he held her hands in one of his, then leaned forward to cup her head with the other, his thumb brushing her cheek. "I love you, Faith Collins, and I don't plan to let you go ever again."

TWENTY-TWO

Faith fought through her headache as she eyed the outline of the two braves riding ahead of her on the trail back to the waterfall. Flies Ahead and Running Bear sat with their hands tied behind them and feet bound beneath each mount's belly. Grant rode with Running Bear's horse tethered to his own, and White Horse held the rope for Flies Ahead's mount.

There was almost no chance these two could get away. Yet Flies Ahead's anger was apparent in the rigid set of his shoulders, and she could still remember the hatred in his eyes as White Horse and Grant secured him on the animal. He would escape if he could possibly find a way. And if he did, his vengeance would have no bounds.

"Almost there." Grant's voice drifted over his shoulder as the sound of the waterfall hummed in the air. "I see the river through the trees."

A weight eased off her chest as the sound of the falls grew louder. They still had decisions to make—what to do with these two kidnappers, and who would go with Grant to find his brother. But at least they were back at the waterfall and cave, where they would have food and protection while they worked through the next plans. And she could finally lie down and close her eyes against the pounding in her head.

She'd felt much better before they left Flies Ahead's camp that morning. But a long day in the saddle, jolting and jostling as the horses climbed and descended slopes, had worsened her pain so much that flashes of light sometimes seared her vision.

Soon, she could rest.

When they rode into the clearing, she caught a glimpse of something that made her gasp. There, near the base of the waterfall, sat three very familiar horses.

She reined around Grant to get a better view, but still, the sight seemed too impossible to believe. "Rosie?"

Her sister was already riding toward them, with Dragoon and Ol' Henry approaching behind her.

A glance sideways showed White Horse had nudged his mount faster, so Faith did the same. Two Bit struck into a canter, maybe as excited to see Rosie's horse as she was to see her sister.

She and Rosie both reined in when they met and jumped to the ground. Her sister might still be angry at her for leaving the way she did, but less than a day ago, she'd thought she would never see her family again. She had to greet Rosie with a hug.

Rosemary met Faith's embrace. She'd been hoping for a bit of warmth in return, but Rosie clutched her so tight tears stung Faith's eyes.

"I'm so glad you're all right," Rosie whispered.

Faith breathed in the feel of her, letting her fear and

worries from the past days fade as she reveled in the love of her sister. A love she'd not realized mattered so very much.

She inhaled the familiar scents that always surrounded Rosie—horse and grass and yes, a bit of sweat. Rosie wasn't afraid of hard work.

When her sister finally pulled away, they both wiped at tears. Rosie shook her head. "We got here as soon as we could. We were worried sick about you."

Rosie's gaze flicked toward the others, catching on White Horse. Even as she couldn't seem to tear her eyes from him, she spoke to Faith. "You have a lot of questions to answer."

Then she moved past Faith to White Horse, who'd dismounted behind Faith's horse. Did Rosie intentionally stop on the other side of Two Bit so the gelding would partially conceal her and White Horse from Faith's view?

She'd sometimes wondered if a special regard might be growing between her sister and White Horse—something more than friendship. The way they stood so close now seemed awfully suspicious. They'd dropped their voices too.

She couldn't see Rosie's face well, but White Horse was looking down at her with as close to a moony-eyed gaze as she'd ever seen from him.

Though she'd love to scoot closer and hear what they were saying, she should allow them a little privacy. Besides, she had other friends to greet.

Ol' Henry and Dragoon stood with their horses, standing back as they waited patiently for their turns. She strode toward them, dragging Two Bit with her. "I never thought I'd see the two of you out here."

She pulled them each into a hug, and Ol' Henry murmured into her hair, "We was worried about you, little sister."

"That's sure 'nuff true." Dragoon wrapped an arm around her, then let her go as he stepped back. He sent a glance toward Rosie. "We stopped at the ranch and happened to mention that we saw Two Bit here at the rendezvous. I said I never thought I'd see the day you sold him. Rosie got all worried about you, an' we went through a heap o' trouble trackin' you down."

She cringed, her headache making itself known once more. "I'm sorry I put you all through that. I found a lead on where Steps Right was, and I had to follow it." Better keep the conversation moving. She turned and motioned for them to follow her. "Let me introduce you to the others."

As they filed past Rosemary and White Horse, the two seemed finished with their quiet conversation and turned to walk with them. Grant had stayed back with both captives and Steps Right.

With Rosie walking beside her, Faith fixed her gaze on the man who'd captured her heart so thoroughly. Grant dismounted and took a few steps forward, but he couldn't leave his charges in order to meet them.

At last, they all halted before Grant. It would be better for her sister to meet Grant first, leaving Steps Right's introduction for the end.

Faith moved to stand partway between her sister and Grant. "Rosie, I'd like to introduce you to Grant Allen. I met him back when I was traveling with Elise and Goes Ahead. He told me about these waterfalls, and when I made up my mind to come search them for Steps Right, he stayed by my side every step of the way. I couldn't have made it without him."

She swallowed, her gaze shifting to meet his. Hopefully

he could see the thankfulness in her eyes. His gaze was warm, but then he shifted back to face Rosie. She should finish her introductions. "Grant, this is my eldest sister, Rosemary." Then she motioned to the men standing behind her. "And our good friends Ol' Henry and Dragoon."

As the men exchanged greetings, Rosie gave Grant a narrow-eyed look and only nodded in response to his "I'm honored to meet you." Then she turned her focus away from him.

Faith's gut twisted at her sister's rudeness. Maybe Faith shouldn't have started the introduction by saying that Grant had been the impetus for Faith to set out on her own. She'd just wanted Rosie to know how vital Grant had been in finding Steps Right. Clearly, they'd need to have a private conversation later.

Rosie also ignored the bound braves, turning her focus to Steps Right. White Horse must have explained their presence here. Had he also told of the kidnapping? Maybe not, or Rosie would have demanded the full story already.

For now, Rosie and White Horse were approaching Steps Right, and quiet had settled over the group entirely.

This felt like White Horse's moment, a time for him to introduce his mother. So Faith stayed back with Grant, sidling a little closer to him as a flutter of nerves eased through her. He must have felt her tension, for his hand moved to her back, imparting a solid strength that eased her churning middle.

This was a happy event. Nothing to worry about.

White Horse spoke with a voice deep and strong enough to mark the moment. "Rosemary Collins. My mother, Steps Right. *Áaksíksikka'yiwa Okamo't.*"

Rosie approached Steps Right where she still sat on her horse. With her injured ankle, she'd stayed in the saddle as much as possible on the ride back.

Steps Right held out a hand to Rosie, and Rosie took it in both of hers. From this distance, Faith couldn't hear her sister's soft words. But Steps Right seemed pleased with them, for the lines on her face curved in a full smile.

"I hear good of you, Rosemary Collins. From my son." Her gaze slipped to White Horse, then dipped back to Rosie.

White Horse looked more sheepish than she'd ever seen him, and even Rosie stepped back, a little flustered. There definitely must be more between them than friendship.

Grant spoke up, his voice a calming blanket over the group. "Why don't we make camp and unload the horses?"

Faith nodded. "We have plenty to eat in the cave. I'll bet you're all hungry."

As the sun dipped below the horizon, they set up a large camp beside the river, a little ways down from the waterfall, where the thunder of water wasn't so loud. Steps Right, Rosie, and Faith would sleep in the cave, but the men would sleep out here.

It would be nice to have some privacy, and these trees provided a better place to tie the braves. They still needed to sort through what should be done with them, but they had too much else to catch up on.

For now, though, they were all sharing the meal around this large campfire. Eating had finally made her headache ease, which was a blessed relief. Between the food their newcomers brought, what was left from Flies Ahead's camp, and a few supplies Steps Right had in the cave, they were enjoying a wide variety of food. Everything from beans and biscuits to *depuyer*, a food White Horse had spoken of in the past as something he missed from his tribe. He'd made it sound like a type of bread, but none of them had been able to learn how to make it.

Now that Faith had sampled a slice, it seemed like a cross between smoked meat and bread pudding. Not easy to describe, but sweet and tender. White Horse had eaten three servings of it so far.

Besides eating, he sat quietly, his mother on one side and Rosie on the other. Rosie had assigned Faith the spot on her other side, probably so she could interrogate her with questions about the kidnapping and the entire journey. Faith had already relayed the main details, skimming over much of the time in Flies Ahead's camp, but it could take days to remember all the things that had happened since she left the ranch with Goes Ahead and Elise and their family. Had that only been a little over a month ago? It seemed a lifetime.

She'd been impulsive and naïve back then. She might still be those things, but hopefully she'd gained wisdom on this journey. She'd certainly added experience.

A glance sideways at Grant eased the tension inside her. He was smiling at something Dragoon said, a tale about the first time Dragoon had spotted her and her sisters at the rendezvous three years ago, back when they'd just come west in search of Steps Right.

"We traveled up and down the Green River Valley for weeks looking for you, ma'am." He turned this remark to Steps Right. "It was quite a mystery where you'd gone."

The older woman didn't show whether she understood

every word, but she seemed to be following the conversation, a constant smile on her face.

Sparks danced skyward from the crackling flames as the group settled into a moment of quiet. Maybe this would be a good time to tease White Horse a little and help Steps Right join the conversation.

Faith straightened. "I've enjoyed hearing Steps Right's stories about White Horse. She told us one about the first time he went hunting with his father." She slid a look at him to make sure she wasn't overstepping her bounds by sharing it with the full group.

His eyes had narrowed a little, but he didn't look angry.

It was Rosie who snatched her focus, though. Her sister tipped her head, a curious expression on her face. "Do you mean the time he sneezed?"

Faith drew back. "How did you know?"

Rosie turned sheepish. "I . . ." She looked to White Horse, out of reflex probably. But the glance made it clear who had told her that story. Her cheeks reddened, but she motioned for Faith to continue. "Go ahead. Tell it for the others."

"Actually, I think Steps Right should tell it." Faith sent the woman a hopeful look.

Steps Right nodded and began the tale as she'd told it in the cave.

Faith took the opportunity to watch her sister from the corner of her gaze. How close were she and White Horse, that he had shared such an intimate story with her? He'd always seemed so much like an older brother to Faith— wise, patient, skilled at nearly everything he attempted. Even teasing at times, in his own way.

White Horse was handsome, no question about that.

And he'd proven his character a thousand times over in the years they'd known him. Rosie was of an age that would be a good match for him. Why had she never considered all this?

Rosie must have felt her looking, for she turned raised brows to her. Faith smiled, trying not to show what she'd been thinking.

Her sister's expression softened, turning sweet and a bit motherly. She leaned close and slipped an arm around Faith's shoulders, speaking just loud enough for Faith to hear. "I'm so glad you're safe."

Faith rested her head on Rosie's shoulder. "I am too."

The stories continued a while longer, and they coaxed Steps Right into sharing several more memories of her family, including from her own girlhood.

If only Lorelei and Juniper could hear these tales. There would be time, though. Once they all reached the ranch, they would be able to draw many more memories from Steps Right, especially through the winter months they would spend in the warm cabin.

As the evening waned, Grant's attention seemed to drift away from their little group. Thinking about finding his brother, most likely. She needed to talk with him. Needed to know what he was thinking. One thing she knew for certain—she wouldn't be sending him off by himself this time.

She also still had to talk with Rosie about Grant. They hadn't had a second alone for that conversation. But it would help to know Grant's plans—and let him know about hers—so she could prepare her sister for this final leg of their trip.

Perhaps Grant overheard her thoughts, for he leaned close and murmured, "Would you like to walk with me?"

She nodded as she met his gaze. He still looked at her with a kind of gentle affection, though his eyes had an extra line or two beneath them. Or was that a trick of the shadows?

When she leaned close to Rosie to share their plans, her sister eyed her warily. "Should I come with you?"

Faith fought to keep from rolling her eyes and instead touched Rosie's shoulder, meeting her sister's focus squarely. "He's a good man, Rosie. I'll tell you more about him when we have time, but you needn't worry."

Rosemary shot a look toward Grant, then pinched her mouth as she gave a single nod. "Call if you need anything."

Faith chuckled as she stood and turned to follow Grant outside of the ring of firelight. Likely, the others were watching them leave, though Dragoon was still bending White Horse's ear about a group of Blackfoot he'd met at this year's rendezvous.

As they settled into the path beside the river's edge, the rustle of the water replaced the murmur of voices behind them.

The quiet didn't last for long. Grant ran a hand through his hair. "I have to go find Will."

As she'd expected. "When do you want to leave?"

They stopped walking, and he turned toward the river. She could barely see his face in the glow of the moonlight. "Now that your sister's here and I know you're safe, I plan to leave in the morning."

She would have liked to have more time to catch up with Rosie, but they could do that later. She nodded. "I'm going with you this time. We'll leave at first light?"

He spun to face her, then regarded her for a moment. If

only the clouds weren't covering so much of the moon and she could see his expression.

At last he said, "I don't imagine your sister will approve of us going off unchaperoned."

She shrugged. "She's welcome to come along if she likes." Or . . . would he rather have privacy when he saw his brother again for the first time after so long?

She touched Grant's arm to stop him, then moved in front of him so she could better see his face in the moonlight. As she spoke, she studied his eyes, searching for a sign of his true thoughts. "I want to be there with you, Grant. But if you'd rather go alone, I won't force my presence on you."

His mouth curved in a gentle smile, but a moment passed before he answered. "If you're willing to go, it would mean a lot to have you there. And I'd like the chance to get to know your sister better if she'll ride with us."

A grin filled her heart, spilling over onto her face. "Good."

Finally, he did what she'd been hoping he'd do all day. He raised his hands to cup her shoulders, then lowered his mouth and kissed her.

TWENTY-THREE

Grant opened his eyes in the darkness, straining to make sense of where he was and what had awakened him. They were in the camp beside the river—all the men in their group. The fire had burned low, casting dim light on the faces of those sleeping around it.

He shifted to look at the two captives tied to the trees at the edge of the camp, able to lie down but not move far. From what he'd heard, that was far more comfort than Flies Ahead had allowed Faith and Steps Right.

He could see Running Bear's form closest to him. But . . .

He sat upright to see Flies Ahead. The place where the brave had lain was empty. No shadowed lump. Not even the blanket.

His heart surged, and he spun to look around them, half expecting to see the brave skulking in the dark to attack.

But there was no sign of him.

"White Horse." Grant reached for his rifle and positioned his gun so he could aim and shoot quickly.

White Horse sat up, his blanket falling aside.

Grant pointed the gun toward the empty ground. "Flies Ahead is gone."

White Horse sprang to his feet, and before Grant could do the same, Ol' Henry's voice whispered from the other side of the fire. "What's wrong?"

He stood and scanned the darkness, moving in the opposite direction from where White Horse had begun to search. He stepped sideways to avoid Running Bear's bound form. "Flies Ahead is—"

The shadows in front of him came alive, and Grant stumbled backward, raising his gun to aim against the unseen threat. Running Bear. How had he come untied?

A feral snarl rumbled through the air, cut off by the blast of a rifle as the shot lit the night. Grant's vision flashed as his mind scrambled to catch up with what had happened.

The gunshot had come from White Horse's direction, and even now, White Horse leapt to the fallen brave's side. The injured man lay curled into a ball as he moaned. White Horse scooped up a knife from beside him. That must be how the braves got loose, but how did they obtain the blade?

Grant spun to scan the area. *Flies Ahead.* Where was he? He must have cut his own ropes, then freed his compatriot. Had he already escaped?

Another thought surged in, this one making him whirl toward the cave. "The women!"

He sprinted toward the falls, footsteps thundering behind him. Were all the men coming with him? Maybe someone should have stayed with Running Bear, but he couldn't worry about that right now.

Flies Ahead was a far bigger threat.

An image slipped in his mind of the way the brave's eyes

had flashed with hatred as they tied him on his horse. There had been murder in his gaze. He wouldn't be swayed from killing Steps Right. And maybe the other women if he could. Rosemary. *Faith.*

He reached the boulders that lined the river leading to the falls. In the darkness and with the mist, he could make out no sign of Flies Ahead. Was the man lurking in the trees somewhere? Watching them? Waiting to pick them off with a stolen gun?

He couldn't slow down to search the woods yet. He had to make sure the women were safe first.

"Quick!" White Horse's sharp call drove Grant forward, and he jumped onto the first boulder.

He'd picked his way through here so many times, he knew where the slippery places were. White Horse would know the same, but not Dragoon or Ol' Henry.

He slowed long enough to call back to them, "Be careful." It looked like the trappers were already slowing to maneuver the rocks. Good.

He refocused on getting to the falls, leaping through the thin curtain of water at the edge. He landed on the ledge behind the falls but had to wait for his eyes to adjust to the darkness.

A shadow moved in the distance, near the cave opening.

Grant charged forward. "Stop!" Not that he expected the brave to halt at his command, but it would warn the women.

Behind him, White Horse yelled too, but in the high-low cadence of the Blackfoot language.

From inside the cave, a scream echoed.

"Faith!" He couldn't tell for sure if it was her, but he had to get to her.

As he rounded the corner into the cave opening, he slipped on a wet spot. He scrambled to catch his footing and pushed into the thick darkness.

Flies Ahead could be lying in wait for them anywhere. In the depths of the cave, all had fallen quiet.

Lord, don't let them be hurt. He pushed aside the image that tried to crowd in of all three women massacred. *Protect them, Lord.*

He kept pushing forward, feeling ahead as he maneuvered the pitch-black corridor. "Faith? Is Flies Ahead in there?"

Before he could hear her answer, a shadow jumped out at him. He lifted his rifle to block the blow, but a powerful force slammed into him, knocking him onto his back.

It had to be Flies Ahead. Grant struggled to push the body off him.

Fire burned along his upper arm. From a knife?

Scuffling sounded, and Flies Ahead moved away from him. That had to be White Horse's doing, but Grant could see nothing in the thick darkness.

He yelled a warning. "A knife! He has a knife."

A string of sounds grunted. Peigan words, maybe, in Flies Ahead's voice. The noise gave Grant a location for their enemy. He needed to help White Horse. The two men must be wrestling.

The scuffling noises moved toward the waterfall, even as Grant tried to find Flies Ahead.

He stepped farther forward, toward the water, trying to catch up to the pair. Trying to help. White Horse must be moving the brave out of the cave, where they would have a better chance. Did he have the upper hand, then?

At last, Grant could see the struggling figures outlined by

the dim light outside. The two were crouched, their arms intertwined. Flies Ahead fought on the right, and Grant charged toward him with the same force the man had used when he first struck Grant.

His blow pushed Flies Ahead farther out onto the ledge, but not as much as he'd hoped. The man had a grip on White Horse, dragging the brave with him.

God, help us!

Flies Ahead hadn't released White Horse, and both men still grunted. He couldn't be certain, but it looked like they gripped each other's necks. He had to help White Horse.

His rifle had been dropped in the chaos in the corridor, but he didn't dare leave White Horse long enough to search for it. He spotted Dragoon and Ol' Henry maneuvering toward them on the ledge, and Dragoon held a rifle.

Grant scooted toward them. "Quick, hand me your gun."

It was too dark and the men too entangled for him to shoot, but if he could knock Flies Ahead unconscious . . .

White Horse released a hard grunt, sending Grant's pulse into a panic.

The moment Dragoon placed the stock in his hand, he gripped the weapon in a tight hold and slammed the butt into Flies Ahead.

A shout rose above the roar of the water, then Flies Ahead stilled.

White Horse pulled away, sagging to the stone floor as his shoulders heaved. He was conscious and moving. *Thank you, God.*

Flies Ahead's body tipped toward the water. His head had slumped, hanging limp. Grant reached for him, but he didn't move fast enough.

Flies Ahead tumbled over the edge.

Grant dropped to his knees and peered down at the river. The churning water where the falls met the river dragged Flies Ahead under, pulling him into its turmoil.

Grant sucked in a breath, his own body losing strength with the realization that the danger might be over. Beside him, White Horse rose up to his knees to peer down too. Grant raised his voice over the water. "He was unconscious when he fell. Do you think he could survive that?"

"We'll go out and make certain." Dragoon reached for his rifle, and Grant handed it over. "We'll check the other fella too."

As the men retreated along the ledge, Grant sank back onto his heels. His heart still raced, and he sucked in breath after breath, his body craving even more.

Then Faith was at his side, slipping her hand around his waist. He wrapped both of his arms around her and pulled her tight.

"Are you hurt?" Her mouth was so close to his ear, she didn't have to yell to be heard.

He soaked in the warm solidness of her, letting it finally slow his frantic pulse. "No." The sting on his arm from the knife wasn't worth mentioning. "Are you? The others?"

"No. We heard you yell before anything happened."

Thank you, God. And he meant those words with every part of his being.

TWENTY-FOUR

Midmorning light shone over the mountains as Faith rode beside Grant the next day, with Rosie, Ol' Henry, and Dragoon trailing behind. Finally, they were headed toward the cabin where Will should be.

The forest canopy formed a tunnel of dappled sunlight around them, the trail through the trees wide enough through here that they could ride two abreast. To their left, the river flowed with a melody that soothed her. Beyond the water rose the peaks, their tops hidden by a wreath of clouds, adding a sense of grandeur to the scene.

Behind her, Ol' Henry was telling a story about the time he'd helped another trapper friend cut trees to build a cabin one winter. The man had planned to go back to St. Louis for his wife and children once he had the home built, but Ol' Henry never knew if he'd accomplished that dream. Once they had the final beams hoisted, Ol' Henry set off to join up with Jim Bridger's trapping party farther downriver.

Dragoon rode quietly in the rear of their group, probably as spellbound by the way Ol' Henry told the tale as they all

223

were. White Horse and Steps Right had stayed behind in the camp near the waterfall.

They'd spent yesterday recovering from the events of the night before. Burying the two braves, doing laundry in the river, cooking a hearty evening meal . . . but mostly grieving the loss of two men who'd been crafted and loved by God but whose lives had ended in such a tragic way. With their passing, the threat to Steps Right was over, and the uncertainty of what to do with their prisoners had resolved itself. The combination of sadness and relief had left them all at ends yesterday.

They had to keep moving, though, so this morning, the five of them had set out on the one remaining mission, the final goal of the journey. They'd ridden three hours so far. Hopefully, having Rosie, Ol' Henry, and Dragoon along helped distract Grant from his worries about how his brother would greet him. But his silent focus still showed in the hard line of his jaw and the wrinkle between his brows.

This should be a joyous occasion—the reuniting of brothers after so many years. She would do everything in her power to make it so, especially lifting their worries to the only One who could really make a difference. *Please, God. Let Will be happy to see Grant.*

An hour later, the trees opened into a clearing bathed in sunlight. The river lined one side of the open ground, and a small cabin sat at its center, a trail of smoke rising from the chimney. The worn logs bore the dark coloring of time and weather, which meant it must have been built long before last summer when Will came west.

She glanced at Grant, who'd slowed his horse but still rode toward the structure. He'd lost some of his coloring, and she had a feeling the sweat dripping down the side of his face wasn't just from the sun. She eased Two Bit a little closer to Grant's gelding. A reminder that they were in this together.

Ahead, there was no sign of movement or sound from the cabin. Did Will still live here? It was hard to tell from the uneven growth of grass. They halted a few steps in front of the cabin. Grant dismounted first, his boots crunching in the dry grass. "Wait here," he said softly.

She reached for his reins, then sent up another prayer as he approached the cabin door.

"Will?" His voice rang louder, holding a tone both friendly and curious. It didn't sound nervous, not that she could detect.

The door creaked open, revealing a man with sun-bronzed skin and a scruffy blond beard that matched his tousled curls. His eyes, the same deep blue as Grant's, eyed him with confusion and uncertainty. As recognition dawned on his face, those eyes widened in surprise and disbelief.

"Will?" The hope in Grant's voice was impossible to miss. "It's me, Grant. Your . . . brother."

Will was already striding from the cabin, nearly tripping as he stepped into the grass, then bracing a hand against the cabin wall behind him. "Grant? Is it really . . . ?"

"It is." A bit of uncertainty crept into Grant's voice, and it made Faith's heart ache. But Grant continued, "You were young the last time I saw you. It's all right if you don't recog—"

Will straightened, pushing away from the wall. "Of course I do, Grant. I just . . . It's hard to believe . . ."

Relief eased Grant's features, and he looked like he wasn't

sure whether he should give his brother a hug or shake his hand or . . . He must have settled on a handshake, and Will took his outstretched grip with both of his, shaking heartily.

"I just can't believe it." He shook his head. "How did you get here?"

A smile was beginning to spread across Grant's face, as though he was finally believing the reality himself. "I'll tell you everything. But first, I want you to meet my friends."

Will turned, and Grant stepped beside him for the introductions.

Faith slid to the ground and moved in front of the horses, and the others did the same. She couldn't help a smile herself. *Thank you, Lord.*

Grant moved toward Faith, drawing her to his side. "Will, this is Faith Collins. I met her when I first started looking for you. We've had quite a journey since then."

Her cheeks were probably turning pink as heat flushed her neck. "It's an honor to meet you, Will." Should she have called him Mr. Allen? Or did he go by the surname of the family who'd raised him? *Will* was probably safest, though not as polite. Hopefully he'd excuse her lack of formal manners.

"I'm pleased to meet you." Will's grin deepened, so genuine and so much like Grant's, it made her chest ache. "Whatever you had to do to bring Grant here, I owe you a debt of gratitude."

Thankfully, Grant saved her a response by motioning to the others. "This is Miss Rosemary Collins, Faith's sister. And friends of the family, Ol' Henry and Dragoon."

Ol' Henry was eyeing Will, and when she glanced back at the younger man, he was doing the same. The old trapper spoke first. "Was you trappin' with Larkin's group last fall? Headin' toward the Snake River?"

Will's head bobbed. "I was. You spent a few days with us, didn't you?"

Ol' Henry's teeth flashed in a grin as he elbowed Dragoon. "That was when you went by the tradin' post an' I stayed with my lame horse."

Will grinned at both trappers, then included Rosie. "I'm honored to meet you all. Overcome, really." His gaze moved back to Grant and hovered for a moment. It almost looked like his eyes grew misty.

Then he stepped and waved for them to follow. "Come on in, everyone. The cabin's not big, but I've had beaver stew cookin' all morning."

After they secured their horses, they followed Will into the small structure. The inside was dimly lit, with an open room that served as a kitchen, bedchamber, and living space. A small table and chair sat in one corner near the fireplace, and piles of furs and other belongings lay scattered around the edges of the room. The air was thick with the scent of woodsmoke and the musky scent of furs.

Will swiped a stack of pelts off a second chair and placed them on a crate. "Settle in. I'll scoop up the stew." He crossed to the fire, where a kettle hung from a tripod, and reached for two of the tin cups hooked on nails protruding from the wall. "It's not much, but it'll stave off hunger."

As he stirred the stew in the pot, Faith spoke up. "We have cornmeal and grease. How about if I make johnnycakes to go with it? Coffee too."

Will looked up, his entire face brightening as he took in her words. "Coffee? That sounds real good."

She and Rosie headed out to retrieve the supplies she'd need. When they returned, the others were perched on mounds of furs. While the men talked, she and Rosie set to work by the fire. Rosie began the batter for johnnycakes, while Faith prepared the coffee.

Will was saying, "I'm makin' do. I hunt and trap. There's plenty of game on the river."

"What made you come west?" Grant's voice sounded calm and interested.

"Wanted to see what all those people comin' through St. Louis were talkin' about." His grin lingered in his voice.

Did he like living so far away from the rest of the world? She wouldn't mind settling in a cabin on the river with so many majestic mountain views, if only it weren't quite so far from her family.

She positioned the coffeepot in the coals as Will spoke again. "Started off with trappin', then kept movin' until I found this place. Gives me a shelter from the weather. Plenty of food around. A good life."

A slight pause lingered, and she worked to keep from turning to see what the men were doing.

Grant broke the quiet, his voice lower than before. "I'm sorry it took me so long to find you. I looked in St. Louis when I could. Never knew where you lived. Then when I was grown, well . . ."

Her heart ached for all he'd gone through, and she held her breath to see how much he would share.

"Things were busy for a while. But last winter, I finally had a chance to search in earnest. I found Mr. Sheldon. He told me you'd gone west in the spring. I'd missed you by less than a year."

Silence settled between them, awkward and clumsy. As she held the frying pan for Rosie to pour circles of batter, she glanced back at them. The brothers were staring at each other. From this angle, she couldn't read their expressions.

Let this be a time of healing for them both, Lord. Give Grant wisdom and strength.

Even with the warm reception they'd received, this might be hard on Will, having his brother show up out of the blue. Maybe he'd thought Grant dead. Or that Grant had given up searching for him. Or *chosen* not to find him. He might have thought he'd been utterly abandoned.

Tears burned her eyes as that possibility took hold.

Grant spoke again. "I'm glad I found you, finally. We have time to catch up." Then his voice changed to a lighter tone. "Faith and her sisters own a ranch near the Green River. Have you seen it?"

Those words lightened the tone, and by the time the food was ready, Ol' Henry and Dragoon had filled in the details about the ranch and Tanner's trading post. As they ate, Will asked them questions about their journey and the men from Parson's group he'd met before. Then came the news about Steps Right, and the concern in his gaze made her love this little brother of Grant's even more than she'd hoped to.

Thank you, Lord. He'd answered her prayers even more abundantly than she'd allowed herself to hope.

TWENTY-FIVE

As the last rays of the sun shone through the open cabin door that evening, Grant sat with his brother at the table in the cabin. Faith and Rosemary had cooked another hearty meal, and now they'd gone with Dragoon and Ol' Henry to the river to wash dishes and enjoy the sunset. Probably they'd stayed gone so long to give him and Will time alone.

It still didn't quite seem real that he was sitting here across from Will. Across from a man who looked enough like him to strike a chord but was his own man. His little brother, now grown enough to live by himself in this cabin so far away from the rest of the world. Will no longer needed a big brother to protect him.

Grant let out a sigh. He'd missed so much of Will's life. But he was here now, and he would make up for lost time.

He followed his brother's glance out the door, where he had a perfect view of the flowing water. "This river reminds me of the one near the old house." He looked over at his brother, recalling the story Will told Steps Right. "Do you remember that mill? We used to go there every day in the summer, swimming and fishing till the sun went down."

Lines creased the edges of Will's eyes. "I remember being scared of that river."

Grant studied him, squinting as he tried to recall that. "Really? Maybe. I remember pushing you in. Mayhap that's what it took to get you over your fear."

Will chuckled, but then his expression turned sober. "So . . . what are your plans now? You said you came west to find me. It seems like you might have found more than you'd been looking for." He nodded toward the open doorway, likely meaning Faith and the others beyond it.

A knot formed in Grant's throat. "You're right." He'd not wanted to face this so soon, but they did need to make some decisions. "Faith and her sister need to get back to their ranch. We left Steps Right and her son, White Horse, at the waterfall, but they'll ride with us to the ranch." He fought to keep from fidgeting as he asked his question. "Would you want to go too? I hate to part with you so soon. It'd likely be about a week's travel, then I hear the ranch is in a pretty valley. I think you'd be welcome to stay as long as you like. Or just a few days if you felt you needed to get back right away."

His brother's eyes had taken on an expression Grant couldn't decipher. Longing? Memory? Indecision? Should he offer to stay here with Will and let the others ensure Faith returned home safely?

Everything in him revolted at the thought. White Horse, Ol' Henry, and Dragoon could likely ensure Faith reached the ranch with little problem, along with Rosemary and Steps Right.

And God. God was the only one who could keep any of them truly safe.

But Grant wanted to be with her. To do everything he could to help and protect her, and to experience the journey at her side.

Was it more responsible to stay here with Will, though, now that he'd finally found him? He had no doubt Faith would understand if he promised to come a week or so later. He didn't even know where the ranch was, but she could give him the directions.

His chest ached at the thought of going that long without seeing her smile. Hearing her bubbling laugh. Kissing her.

Will nodded decisively, drawing him back to the present. Could his brother see where his thoughts had wandered?

"I can ride along too. I promised Steps Right I'd come check on her before the trees started to turn, and I can't let her leave the area without saying g'bye." His eyes twinkled. "It'll be good to make sure she's settled in and has all she needs. And see the ranch where you'll be setting up house."

Heat flared up Grant's neck, and he shook his head. His brother wasn't far off with that assessment, but he couldn't let him get ahead of things. "Faith and I don't have an understanding." *Yet.*

Will raised his brows. "But you're planning to ask her, right?"

Grant nodded. "When we get to the ranch and things settle down."

Will nodded, as though he'd assumed as much. "Sounds like I need to be there, then." He pressed his hands against the table's edge and stood. "Guess I better get packed up. I'll be ready to ride out in the morning."

Relief eased through Grant like a cool breeze on a sweltering day. "Thank you, Will. You coming means more than you know."

⟨❧⟩

This was the moment Faith had been waiting for for more than three years now.

One of the moments, anyway.

She rode next to Grant, his brother on his opposite side, though Will had dropped behind a little as the trail narrowed through this pass. Rosie, White Horse, and his mother clustered behind them. All of them were eager to see the ranch buildings spread out in the valley below. Dragoon and Ol' Henry had headed toward the trading post to let Lorelei and Tanner know they were home.

Juniper and Lorelei would finally get to meet Steps Right. All four sisters would finally be together with this woman who had made such a difference in their father's life—and in their own, for she'd been the reason they came west. They could give her the beads, finally returning them to the family where they belonged. God had used that necklace for so much, even more than she could fathom right now.

If they hadn't come west, Juniper would have never met Riley, and sweet little Bertie wouldn't be alive today. They wouldn't have these good friends, Ol' Henry and Dragoon. Lorelei would never have met Tanner.

And White Horse . . . she couldn't imagine not having this honorary brother as part of their family. Would Rosie make him an even closer member one day soon? She fought a grin at the thought. Did Lor and June know? Surely Faith hadn't been the only one unaware of what their elder sister was hiding.

She slid her gaze to the man sitting tall beside her, and a rush of love stung her eyes. If she'd never come west, if she'd never set out with their missionary friends to find Steps Right on her own, she would never have met Grant. Her life was so much fuller with him in it.

He must have felt her gaze, for he looked over at her. That warmth lit his eyes, the expression he saved only for her. Again, tears burned. Happy tears. *Thank you, Lord. Thank you for Grant. And for so much more.*

They were cresting the ridge now, and the ranch would spread out in the valley below them. With the sun in the midafternoon position, Riley would likely be out with the horses, as long as Juniper hadn't developed the same sickness with this babe that she had when she was carrying Bertie.

As the ranch spread out before them, she inhaled a deep breath of the familiar air. The animals started down the slope, and part of her wanted to kick Two Bit into a run, as she had so many times.

But she didn't want to leave Grant behind. She wanted to experience this reunion with him.

The main cabin and barn sat nearest them, with corrals fanning out. Then White Horse's lodge, and Riley and Juniper's cabin. A figure was just stepping from that door— a small person who toddled out, then plopped onto the ground.

Faith grinned and pointed. "There's little Bertie."

Grant followed the line of her finger. "She's cute."

He wouldn't be able to truly see how adorable those

pudgy cheeks were, for they were still too far away to see her as more than an outline.

He looked at her with raised brows. "This looks like a good area to let the horses stretch their legs. Wanna run?"

Her own smile came quick and free. This man could either hear her thoughts or God had made him a more perfect match for her than she'd thought possible. She loosened Two Bit's reins and nudged his sides. The gelding lunged forward, covering the ground like he was as eager to get home as she was.

When they neared the main house, she slowed him to a walk. Juniper walked out of her cabin and paused to shade her eyes and study them.

Faith waved. "June!"

Her sister's demeanor changed as she dropped her hand, and her teeth flashed in a broad grin. She grabbed up her skirts and started to run toward them. Her belly must already be growing awkward, for she slowed to a walk quickly, then continued with one hand under her middle and a long stride.

Faith pushed her gelding into a trot to cover the last of the distance. When she reached Juniper, she reined in and jumped to the ground in the same motion. Juniper enveloped her in a hug, and Faith wrapped her sister as tight as she could manage. The bulge between them kept them a little apart.

"Oh, Faithie," June murmured, still gripping her close. "We prayed and prayed you'd come home safe."

Tears burned Faith's eyes, so she squeezed them shut. "I'm here." It was all she could manage as she soaked in the love her sister offered so freely. Love she'd known would be here waiting for her.

She'd never realized how blessed she was to have this family. A family that clung together no matter what they faced. Just before she pulled back, she sniffed to clear her tears. It wouldn't do for Juniper to see her crying.

But June's smile seemed to say she knew and understood. She moved her grip to Faith's elbow and used her skirt to wipe her own eyes. "I'm a waterworks these days."

"Ah!"

A little voice behind them made Faith turn. "Bertie." She released her sister and turned to swoop up her precious niece. She squeezed her tight, breathing in the sweet little-girl scent. "Auntie Faith missed you so much."

Bertie didn't speak, but she wrapped her pudgy arms around Faith's neck. They both turned to watch as Juniper approached Grant. He'd dismounted to wait quietly while Faith greeted her sister. Rosie was bringing in the rest of the group at a more sedate pace. Probably giving Faith this moment in private.

Faith stepped forward, Bertie still snuggled in her arms. "Juniper, you get to be the first to meet Grant Allen. He's been . . ." How in the world could she sum up all he'd done and become to her? "Well, I couldn't have managed this journey without him."

Juniper's gaze slid to her face. Though Faith kept a cheery smile in place, Juniper surely saw—or suspected—at least some of what Faith wasn't saying. About Grant . . . and about the journey.

Juniper extended her hand. "It's a pleasure to meet you, Mr. Allen. I'm Juniper Turner."

Grant accepted her outstretched hand and bowed over it, a formal side of him Faith hadn't seen. It only deepened her grin, especially when he said, "I've been eager to meet you, Mrs. Turner. Your sisters and friends have told me so much about you all. I hope you don't mind my brother and I have tagged along." He glanced over his shoulder, where Will was riding up with Rosie and the others.

Their approach drew June's attention from answering Grant as she studied the newcomers. Could she see Steps Right riding beside White Horse? Did she know who she was? Faith could barely keep from blurting out the news, but she needed to wait for this first meeting to be done right.

Faith sent a glance toward the distant herd behind Juniper and murmured, "Is Riley with the horses?"

June nodded, still not taking her eyes from the approaching group.

When they all reined in, Rosie and White Horse helped Steps Right down from her mount, then White Horse helped his mother hobble forward. Days in the saddle had slowed her healing, but she moved around better now than when they'd first found her. White Horse looked to Faith, like he wanted her to make the introduction.

She swallowed down the lump in her throat. "Juniper, this is Steps Right, White Horse's mother and the woman who saved our father's life more than two decades ago."

Juniper approached her reverently, taking Steps Right's hands in her own. "I'm so honored to meet you. I'm Juniper. We've been searching . . ." Her voice broke, and the two simply stood together, hands clasped. After a moment, Juniper sniffed again and turned to Faith. "You brought her home. Finally."

Faith nodded, emotion clogging her throat and burning her eyes. They all had. She met Rosie's gaze, where she stood on the other side of Juniper. Her oldest sister smiled at her with glistening eyes. A smile that held so much warmth and pride, it felt just like a hug.

Juniper laughed, sniffing once more as she looked over at Rosie. "Someone should go for Lor and Tanner."

Rosie nodded. "Ol' Henry and Dragoon already have. I expect they'll all be here in an hour or two."

Juniper gave a firm nod. "Good." She grinned at Steps Right for another moment, then released the older woman's hands and turned to White Horse. She pulled him into a hug, laughing again.

White Horse looked more than a little uncomfortable with the sudden outpouring of physical affection. Faith couldn't help chuckling, especially when Steps Right patted her son's shoulder, her own grin spreading wide. Though White Horse felt very much like the brother they'd always wanted, none of them had actually given him a hug, as far as she could remember. Maybe motherhood had freed June to demonstrate her fondness more openly.

When Juniper released White Horse, Faith directed her attention toward Will, who'd lingered behind them all. "This is Grant's brother, Will. Grant came west to look for him, and we found him in a little cabin on the Shaheela River, about a half day's ride from the cave where Steps Right was staying."

Juniper sent her another raised-brow look. "I can't wait to hear the entire story." But then she reached to shake Will's hand. "I'm glad to meet you, Mr. Allen." She slid a confused look toward Grant. "Or should I call you Will?" She was probably trying to determine who was the eldest, for that usually determined who would be called by the surname.

Faith's belly tightened. She'd not determined whether he went by the same name as Grant, or if he'd taken on his adopted family's last name.

Will answered it with a grin. "Just call me Will."

Juniper gave a gracious smile. "Welcome, Will."

Faith turned to Two Bit. "Bertie girl, you wanna ride with me to find your daddy? He needs to come meet everyone too."

When the child bobbed her head enthusiastically, Faith lifted her up onto the front of her saddle, then climbed up behind her. She smiled at the group. "We'll be back."

Her gaze found Grant's, as it usually did, and he sent her a wink. He was such a different person now, ever since the day he and White Horse had rescued her and Steps Right from Flies Ahead's camp. The new life inside him was impossible to miss. They'd prayed together often since then. And the peace on his face when he communicated with the Father made her heart swell every time.

TWENTY-SIX

A glorious sunset of orange and purple streaked the western horizon as they all sat around the campfire outside White Horse's lodge that evening. Steps Right sat as the special guest of honor, with Faith on one side and White Horse on the other. Rosie sat on his left. It was becoming so natural to see the two of them together. Their lingering gazes didn't catch her off-guard anymore.

She hadn't had a chance to ask June or Lorelei whether they knew anything about Rosie's feelings. Too much had happened that day. When Lorelei and Tanner arrived with Ol' Henry and Dragoon, there had been another round of introductions and tears, and they'd begun preparing for this celebration meal.

Faith eyed Lorelei, who sat on Rosie's left across the fire. She looked radiant, and even had a little bump beneath her dress, though it couldn't be seen the way she sat now. Tanner had his arm braced beside her, giving her something to lean against. He took such good care of Lorelei, adoring her the way she deserved. Faith couldn't imagine a better choice for her sweet sister.

Juniper had found her perfect match too. Apparent now as Riley stood behind his wife, bouncing their overly tired toddler to distract her so Juniper could stay seated with the group. Currently, she'd settled next to Will, peppering him with questions about his time in the west. She'd already done the same with Grant, hearing his retelling of their travels to find Steps Right. Faith had told her sisters the details as they were cooking that afternoon, but they would likely be sharing memorable moments for days to come.

When Will finished answering Juniper's latest question, June glanced around the fire at the group. Faith caught her gaze, and her sister's warm smile eased any lingering tension in her chest. It was so good to be home, surrounded by those who loved her.

Juniper's focus shifted to Rosemary, and a look passed between them. Faith's heart picked up speed. Rosie's glance darted to Steps Right, then she stood and moved back out of the circle of firelight. Was this the moment?

When she and her sisters had gathered this afternoon for her to give the full report of her journey, Rosemary had asked them all if they'd like to present the beads to Steps Right this evening, if the time seemed right. Could there be a moment more perfect than this gathering of friends under the wide expanse of the starry sky?

Rosie returned to the firelight, but this time crouched beside Steps Right. White Horse scooted over so she could settle where he'd been beside his mother. Steps Right regarded her, watching with interest.

Rosemary held the leather pouch in her hands, the one

that had hung around Faith's neck for weeks. The one that had somehow ended up in Grant's saddlebag, bringing him back to her on the day she needed him most.

As though he could feel her thoughts, or maybe because her fingers brushed against his trousers, his hand closed around hers, strong and steady. His grip settled her, and she tightened her hold on him.

The entire group had quieted, and Rosie looked at each of their sisters—Juniper, then Lorelei, then her—before turning back to Steps Right.

Her voice came strong as she focused on the woman. "You once found our father, injured on the plain and near death. You stayed with him, caring for him until help could come. Because of your kindness, he lived to come home to us. To help his daughters grow." Her gaze slid to Faith for a half second as the corners of her mouth tipped. "One of his daughters would never have been born, had you not saved his life."

Faith couldn't help her own smile. In more ways than one, she wouldn't be here without this special woman.

Rosie's fingers slipped into the opening of the pouch in her lap, pulling out the string of blue crystal beads. She raised them to hang from her left hand, then draped them over her right so she extended the necklace like the gift of the magi.

"You gave this to our father that night on the plain, and he told you stories of his family, a story for each bead in this necklace. He would not have lived that night without your care and the hope you gave him through the beads of this necklace."

Steps Right's eyes had begun to glisten, and Rosie's voice

softened as she continued. "Three years ago, as my sisters and I were gathered around him during his final moments on this earth, our father asked us to bring the beads back to you so they could be reunited with the other strands passed down through your family's generations. We're honored to finally accomplish this. But even more than that, we're honored to know you and your son."

A few tears had slipped past Faith's defenses as she listened, and now her blurry vision made her nearly miss the way Rosemary turned to look at White Horse, just for a moment.

Steps Right took the beads from Rosie, then gathered them in one hand and used her free one to reach out and clasp Rosie's fingers. When she spoke, though, she used her Peigan tongue, speaking a string of words to White Horse.

His voice came deeper, softer, as he interpreted. "My mother thanks you for bringing the beads. But she is more thankful for you, her daughters."

Steps Right's eyes smiled as she looked from Rosie on her left to Faith on her right, then to Lorelei and Juniper. She still gripped Rosie's hand, and quietly, she placed the bead necklace in her lap and reached for Faith's also.

As Steps Right's warm palm pressed against her own, Faith gave a gentle squeeze back. Through tears of joy, she let her gaze roam the group of people she loved. Steps Right, her sisters and the men special to them, her niece, their friends. And Grant.

He held her gaze as his thumb stroked the back of her hand. His eyes said everything she needed to know about the depth of his affection.

Thankfulness welled in her so rich and full, new tears

slipped down her cheeks, following the curves of her smile. *Father in heaven, your goodness is far better than I could have imagined.*

When the fire had died down, Grant helped Faith carry the food and dishes that had come from the main cabin, while the others worked through the smaller details to ensure everyone settled in for the night. He and Will had already pitched a tent, as had Dragoon and Ol' Henry. White Horse had made a place for his mother in his lodge, and the rest would sleep in the two cabins.

The day had been so full, arriving at the ranch and meeting all the people who meant so much to her. She was loved abundantly, as he'd known she must be. But what continued to catch him by surprise was how easily they welcomed him in as one of them. Maybe because he'd already met Rosemary and she'd allowed him to come.

He'd expected to have to prove himself to her other sisters and their husbands, as he'd had to with White Horse and Rosemary already. But their focus had mainly been on Steps Right and on Faith, as it should have been.

When he set the last empty crate on the stack under the counter in their kitchen, Grant turned to Faith in the dim light of the cabin she and Rosie shared. "Are you too tired for a walk under the stars?"

He hadn't planned to ask that. She was likely exhausted. But he wasn't ready to leave her yet, even for the night.

She smiled and slipped her hand into his, weaving their fingers together in the intimate way she did sometimes. "I would love that."

As they left the cabin, he turned them toward the river and kept to an easy stroll. The water seemed a natural place for the two of them.

Faith must have felt the same way, for she leaned into his arm. "Why is it you and I always find ourselves near a river when we're together?"

He couldn't help a little teasing. "I suppose you just like being rescued."

She straightened and sent him a look that made his blood heat. "Not hardly."

He chuckled, forcing his body to ignore its impulses. "I well know you can fend for yourself, Miss Collins." He tapped her chin, though touching her proved dangerous. "As I recall, you had to rescue me once or twice also."

Her smile flashed up at him as she kept moving toward the river.

They might always joke about their first meeting, but he loved having so many memories with her. Some thrilling, some that made him smile, and a few he'd rather not relive. He'd always treasure every one.

And speaking of treasures . . . He reached into his pocket and fingered the smooth stone he'd placed there. As they reached the river's edge and listened to the gentle murmur of the flow, he pulled out the stone and held it out to Faith. "I brought you something. From the pool beneath the waterfall where we found Steps Right."

She reached tentatively toward the stone but paused before touching it and looked up at Grant, her eyes hopeful. Did she realize what he meant by it? He'd not expected her to make the connection until he told her, but Faith was so intuitive.

He swallowed. "A memory stone. You said you lost the rocks you collected with your mother. I thought you might want to start a new collection."

Her eyes stayed on his face as he talked, as though reading each word he spoke in his eyes. Her expression shifted from wonder to pleasure, and without breaking her gaze, she closed her fingers around the stone in his hand.

"Grant." She lifted it up, nearly to eye level so she only had to glance sideways to admire it. "This is perfect." Her voice held so much joy, it drew out his own grin.

"I hoped you'd think so."

She leaned up and pressed a kiss to his lips. Just a single, gentle caress, and he had to hold himself perfectly still to keep from wrapping her close and deepening the kiss like everything in him wanted to.

But out here under the stars, so far from her family, she was too much temptation. She deserved for him to be strong.

As she pulled away and turned to the river, he scrambled to make his mind work. He had to find something that would distract his insides. He inhaled a deep breath, then let it out as he lifted his gaze upward.

A familiar sparkle winked down from above. He pointed to the sky. "See those four stars that form a W? They make up the constellation Cassiopeia."

Her teeth flashed in a smile far more appealing than even the stars. "I see it. What's her story?"

Well, that would provide a good distraction. "She was kind of a vain woman, but her daughter's tale is the one you'll probably like. Princess Andromeda was tied to a stone in the ocean when she was attacked by a sea monster."

Her eyes widened. "Who tied her there?"

He shrugged. "That's not really important." And not something suitable for polite conversation. He slid a look her way as he made his tone more dramatic. "What matters to Princess Andromeda is that a brave and valiant warrior named Perseus came along just in time. He fought off the monster and saved the beautiful princess."

She gave him a coy look. "Oh really? Just in time, huh? And how did she reward him for rescuing her?"

Grant turned to face her, drawing her close. She came willingly, and he wrapped his hands around her waist, settling them at the small of her back. "Well, rumor has it she bestowed a kiss on him under the stars. And they lived happily ever after."

She pressed her palms flat against his chest. She could probably feel the way his heart raced under her touch. "They did? Did that kiss go something like this?" She reached up and tipped his chin down with her thumb, then brushed her warm lips across his. She pulled back the tiniest bit, then lingered with a fingertip of space between them. Her breath mingled with his . . . far too much temptation.

He moved his hands from her back, pulling back so he could place his hands over hers. He cupped his fingers around hers, lifting them so he could kiss their tips. "Faith, you're far too much temptation for me. And I want to do this right."

She met his gaze, her mouth curving again even as she put another handsbreadth of space between them. "Is that better?"

He eased out his breath and nodded. Only a little, but he didn't want to frighten her. He would protect her—cherish her—with his last ounce of strength.

As she held his gaze, he did his best to find a way to tell her that. "I love you, Faith Collins."

Her eyes glistened. "And I love you, Grant Allen."

Then she stepped closer and laid her head on his shoulder, and he wrapped her in his arms again. Holding her. Relishing the peace of her in his arms.

Thank you, Lord, for this woman.

When he'd come west, he'd thought all he wanted was to find Will. But God had understood the true desires of his heart, far more than he'd known himself. The Lord had given him abundantly more than Grant had asked for, proving Himself trustworthy over and over.

Lord willing, he and Faith would have a lifetime to see what other surprises their Father had in store for them.

EPILOGUE

The late-summer sun cast a warm glow over the grassy yard beside the main cabin as Grant sat on a quilt between Faith and his brother. The rest of their group stretched out on other blankets, relaxing after their little church service and the hearty meal the women had put together afterward.

Nearly a week had passed since they'd arrived at the Collins ranch, this haven nestled in a wide valley with the distant peaks rising majestically in every direction. No wonder Faith loved this place. He could only pray she'd be agreeable to what he was about to ask.

He glanced around the group once more. Dragoon and Ol' Henry had ridden out a few days ago, but the rest of Faith's family were here, including the honorary Peigan members.

With souls at rest and bellies full, the bright sunshine seemed to be lulling everyone to sleep. Riley and Juniper's little daughter, Bertie, had already succumbed, her body sprawled across the blanket and her small mouth parted to allow even breathing.

A few conversations still carried on, like the one between Will and White Horse, as his brother asked the brave's opinion about some of the land they'd both traveled. Will had the urge to wander, it seemed. Maybe that meant he'd come for regular visits amidst his travels.

When White Horse finished speaking and Will didn't immediately ask another question, Grant prepared himself to speak. This was it.

But before he could get the first word out, Lorelei's voice drifted from the blanket where she lay, her hand shading her eyes. "White Horse, your stories never fail to amaze me."

His mouth curved in a small smile as he sat with his back against a tree. "What is it that surprises you?" Sharing his blanket were his mother, who lay propped against a stack of furs someone had brought out for her, and Rosemary.

"Just that you remember so much about everywhere you've been. The way you just described that bluff, I'd think you stared at it every day for ten years. Most likely, though, you only rode past it one time. Maybe even in the dark."

Now the corners of his eyes crinkled. "It was early morning, but the sun had risen enough for me to see its outline."

Lorelei snorted, and a few chuckles drifted through the group.

Grant should speak up now, before a new conversation began. This would be the last time all of Faith's family were together for many days. Maybe weeks. He had to take this opportunity.

Will cleared his throat like he was about to say something, but Grant sent a sharp elbow into his brother's side.

To cover Will's surprised noise, Grant cleared his own throat and started in. "I have a question."

All eyes turned to him, and he couldn't stop the wave of heat that rose up his neck. He couldn't back down now, though.

He swallowed down his nerves and focused on Rosemary first. "A request, actually. I . . ." He slid a quick look toward Faith. That was a mistake, for her wide eyes nearly made him falter. Was she worried about what he was about to ask?

He tore his gaze away from her and focused on Juniper this time. "From the moment I met your sister, I knew she was special. But the more I've come to know her, the more I realize she's one of the most remarkable women God created."

He shifted his attention to Lorelei. She'd sat upright, and now clasped her husband's hand, her eyes shining. The encouragement on her face made his words come easier. "I didn't realize what I was missing before I met Faith, but now I can't imagine life without her. I'd like to ask her to marry me. But first, I'm asking for your blessing—each of you." He looked to White Horse and met the brave's eyes for an extended breath, then moved his gaze to scan the entire group, touching on Tanner and Riley as well as the women. He wanted all of Faith's family to know he meant this.

Though a sound like a sniffle drifted from Faith's direction, he didn't allow himself to look that way again. Maybe he should have asked her first, but this had felt like the right way to begin. That had come clear the more he prayed for the Lord's guidance.

At last, Rosemary cleared her throat. She slid a look to

Juniper and Lorelei, then to White Horse. Then, finally, she turned her attention to Grant. She straightened her posture and met his gaze.

"We appreciate your request. Faith is"—she sent a small smile to her youngest sister—"special. We won't part with her unless the man will take care of her the way she deserves. A man who loves God and desires to make her happy. Who understands her spirit and will nurture it, not restrict her."

She paused, and his chest ached for breath, but he couldn't draw in air as he waited.

"Speaking for my sisters and the rest of those gathered here, we can't think of anyone better for our littlest sister. You have our blessing."

The relief and elation that washed through him nearly made his vision spin. He struggled for words. "Thank you." It was all he could manage as he breathed in a deep gulp of air.

After two more steady breaths, his mind cleared.

Faith.

He turned to her, and the sight of her made his throat constrict. The sun reflected off the twin tracks of moisture sliding down her cheeks. Her eyes—those beautiful blue windows—shimmered.

He swallowed hard, his heart pounding as he gathered the words she needed to hear. The ones he'd been planning. Why had he thought it right to do this in front of the entire crowd? But Faith deserved this, and he couldn't back down now.

"Faith, the first time I saw you, clinging to that rock by the waterfall, my life was changed. Your strength, determi-

MISTY M. BELLER

nation, and unwavering spirit have drawn me like nothing else. As we've journeyed together, I've found myself falling more and more in love with you." His words tumbled out, raw and honest, leaving him exposed and vulnerable. The world around them faded away, leaving only the two of them.

He reached for Faith's hand and brushed his thumb across the top of it. "You've brought light and love into my life in a way I never thought possible. And I want nothing more than to spend the rest of my days by your side, caring for you, protecting you, and cherishing you as you deserve."

His breath hitched in his throat as he searched her eyes for any sign of hesitation. But only love and warmth reflected back at him.

"Will you marry me, Faith?"

Faith bit her lower lip, trying to contain the grin that threatened to overtake her face. Her heart swelled with happiness—too much joy to contain. Grant was still looking at her, his eyes pleading and hopeful.

"Yes. Of course, yes." Laughter spilled out with the words.

The chorus of squeals and cheering from her family drowned out any response Grant might have uttered, but his grin said plenty. Her own smile had spread all the way to her ears, and she had no plans to stop it any time soon.

As the excited voices settled, Juniper spoke above the others. "I'd say this calls for a celebration. Anyone up for blackberry pie?"

Once more, the chatter rose. Riley pushed to his feet and trotted toward the main house, where June must have left

253

the dessert cooling. While they waited, Faith received hugs from each of her sisters, relishing the love and support from each of them. *This, Lord. This was worth waiting for.*

When Riley returned with the pie, Juniper sliced it quickly and passed out servings. A single pie didn't last long among this group, but the warm confection was worth savoring.

When she finished her last bite, she settled into the crook of Grant's arm with a happy sigh. Juniper was telling the story of Bertie's antics while she'd helped roll out the pie dough, which kept the others distracted.

Grant's warm breath brushed against her ear as he murmured, "Thank you."

She glanced up at him from the edge of her vision. "For what?"

"For saying yes." His eyes twinkled, but she could see the truth behind their teasing.

She squeezed his hand, her heart swelling with affection. "I always will."

He squeezed her back and leaned even closer. "That's what I'm counting on." Then his mouth rested on top of her head, pressing a kiss to her hair that embraced around her like a warm promise.

She had no idea where the journey ahead would take them, but with God leading the way and this man's arms wrapped around her, she couldn't wait to begin.

USA Today bestselling author **Misty M. Beller** writes romantic mountain stories set on the 1800s frontier and woven with the truth of God's love. Raised on a farm and surrounded by family, Misty developed her love for horses, history, and adventure. These days, her husband and children provide fresh adventure every day, keeping her both grounded and crazy. Misty's passion is to create inspiring Christian fiction infused with the grandeur of the mountains, writing historical romance that displays God's abundant love through the twists and turns in the lives of her characters. Sharing her stories with readers is a dream come true. She writes from her country home in South Carolina and escapes to the mountains any chance she gets. Learn more and see Misty's other books at MistyMBeller.com.

For more from

MISTY M. BELLER,

READ ON FOR AN EXCERPT FROM

WARRIOR'S HEART

On assignment to help America win the War of 1812, Evan MacManus is taken prisoner by Brielle Durand—the key defender of her people's secret French settlement in the Canadian Rocky Mountains. But when his mission becomes at odds with his growing appreciation of Brielle and the villagers, does he dare take a risk on the path his heart tells him is right?

Available now wherever books are sold.

Another ten paces and she'd have to shoot.

Brielle Durand steadied the arrow fletching against her cheek, then pushed her body farther into the bow to draw the cord tighter.

The man in her sights rode calmly forward, his breath blowing white in the early morning air. The mount beneath him snorted, releasing its own cloud as it bobbed against the bit. The animal must sense the nearing danger.

In truth, the beast had more intelligence than its rider. As was usual in the ways of animals. Especially when compared to an Englishman like this fellow appeared to be.

Five more strides.

She narrowed her gaze, focusing on the point of aim so her arrow would hit his midsection. Should she give him warning? Perhaps the cry of a mountain lion would plant fear in his chest. She caught her breath, preparing to make the fierce scream she'd practiced so oft.

But the man spurred his horse faster, as though eager to charge through the opening in the rock. Surely he couldn't see the sheltered courtyard just beyond. The place forbidden to outsiders—especially Englishmen.

She locked her jaw to steady herself. Since her eighteenth birthday, when she'd finally been allowed to fight with the warriors, she swore an oath each morning to protect their village. Never again would an Englishman enter their inner circle unhindered. Her people had learned the terrible lesson well the last time. Memory of her mother's lifeless eyes tried to surface, but she pushed the distraction away.

Pressing against the bow, she took a final breath to aim, then let the arrow fly. *Guide its path, Lord.*

A roar broke the morning quiet, radiating from the rocky cliffs like the bellow of a wounded bear. The man doubled over, wrapping his arms around his middle. The long slender shaft of her arrow extended from the leathers that clothed him.

She inhaled a steadying breath, then released it. She'd done what she must to protect her people. Now came the time to uncover his reason for approaching the circle. Her home.

The safety of her people.

◦⊙◦

Evan MacManus gripped the arrow shaft with both hands, forcing his body to draw in air despite the agony in his gut.

He'd not even heard the Indians' approach. Not noticed any quieting of the forest creatures. He must be losing his instincts, and this arrow served as grave proof of that fact.

He reined Granite into a cluster of trees, where the trunks might shield him from another arrow. Precious little time remained to extract the point before the Indians would be upon him. His hammering pulse only made each breath harder to inhale. He had to push aside the pain and focus on what must be done.

Feeling for the solid thickness of the arrowhead to make sure the iron hadn't sunk completely beneath his skin, he clenched his jaw at the cramping in his gut. Best to get this over with.

The arrow pulled loose from his flesh in a clean motion—maybe it hadn't sunk deep enough to damage any organs. The tip snagged on his buckskin tunic, and he wiggled it loose but stopped himself before hurling the wicked thing into the woods. With a hand pressing his undershirt against the wound to stanch the bleeding, he tucked the arrow in his musket scabbard and peered around the trunk of the tree nearest him. He could investigate which tribe had made the weapon later. If he survived this attack. At the moment, he had to find a way to ensure he didn't get a more personal introduction to whoever shot him.

No movement flashed in the morning light beyond the trees. Only a cluster of scraggly bushes marked the other side of the trail. But the warrior had likely been shooting from farther ahead, maybe even from the bend in the path, where the bases of two mountains met to form a narrow opening between them. The gap created a natural gateway where an enemy could find cover and wait.

A spasm seized Evan, doubling him over as he fought to stifle a groan. He had to keep breathing, or this lightness in his head would take over.

"To the ground. Now," barked a voice behind him. The tone held an accent, but not any Indian tongue he'd ever heard.

Evan twisted, biting back a grunt as he tried to focus his wavering vision on the figure standing not five strides behind his horse, bow and arrow at the ready. He had no doubt that second arrow would find its way into his flesh if he didn't obey the order.

Pressing a hand tight against his wound, he clutched his saddle horn with the other and eased himself to the ground. He didn't release his hold on either the saddle or his gut as he tried to settle the spinning in his head. Had he lost so much blood already? The warm liquid coated his hand, which meant he wasn't stopping the flow. Yet he shouldn't be this lightheaded so quickly.

Ignoring the thought, he squinted at the bundle of furs before him.

"To the ground, I said. Or it's another arrow you'll meet."

That was no Indian's speech. Certainly not broken English, but the words contained a lilt only a Frenchman could master.

Blast. How had he stumbled upon the enemy all the way out here? He'd hoped—prayed—this territory was too far west for him to meet one of the Canadians they were fighting.

"Who are you?" He knew better than to argue with a man pointing a weapon, but the cramping in his gut made his thoughts swim in a disjointed flow.

A growl emanated from his adversary. Guttural, but not so deep as he would have expected. Still, the tone made it clear the fellow's patience was fast waning.

Evan released the saddle horn, lowered his arm, and sank to his knees on the frozen ground. Snow hadn't yet fallen in this part of the territory, but if the cold stinging his exposed skin was any indicator, an icy torrent would be upon them soon.

The Indian—or whoever was cloaked in the animal

skins—circled around him, never dropping the aim of his arrow. The faint crackle of leaves bespoke an approach from behind. Would the man bind his wrists or pierce him with a knife and end his life?

Evan would have to turn and topple the stranger if he were to have any chance of getting the upper hand. He could do it, even with the arrow wound, certainly. He'd fought tougher opponents in battle after having received more than one slice from a saber. A Frenchman would be an easy match—if only he could keep his swirling wits about him.

Footsteps padded behind him, and Evan tensed to spin and strike.

"Lower your—"

He whirled and shot his fist forward, praying his aim would be true, even though his target blurred into three shapes. His arm struck something—fur?—and the man issued a high-pitched gasp. Was this a boy?

But Evan had no time to ponder as something grabbed his wrist and a force slammed into his back, shoving him down, almost to the ground.

He writhed, jerking his arm to get away from the man's grasp. Evan brought his free hand around to strike a blow. The effort sent a knife of pain through his gut, but he clamped his jaw tight and fought harder.

His opponent moved too quickly, out of striking distance before Evan could land a blow. His dizziness must be slowing his movements, but he had to overcome that. The man had Evan's arm pinned behind him now, and a boot in his back, pressing him toward the dirt.

He resisted the pressure, his stomach hovering about a foot above the forest floor. But the effort stole his strength more every second. He'd have enough energy left for one more counterattack, and this time he had to overcome his enemy or he'd never complete his mission. He'd already spotted signs that he might have reached his goal.

This mountain he'd been riding around possessed the orange striations usually found near pitchblende. Now he had to locate that mineral itself so the army's scientists could create the blast that would finally end this brutal war. This work was all he had left, and he'd carry out his assignment no matter what it took.

Somehow, he had to make restitution for last time.

With a mighty effort, he twisted around, reaching for the ankle that held him low. The attacker must have been prepared for his movement and grabbed Evan's free wrist, jerking his hand upward so his arms burned at the joint of his shoulders—effectively stealing the last of his strength and gaining the upper hand. Literally.

Were these his final moments? They couldn't be. *God, help me.*

Evan knelt there, struggling for breath. Even when he sucked in air, the wind didn't seem to satisfy the craving in his chest. Perhaps the arrow had punctured his breathing vessel.

His captor worked quickly with his wrists, wrapping a rough cord around them. Despite the unsteadiness in his head, Evan strained to look around, to keep his ears aware of any sound that might give notice of more enemies approaching. Perhaps help, even, as unlikely as that was. But one could hope.

No unnatural noises greeted him. Only a pheasant's call broke the cold silence.

At last, the man behind him gave a final jerk on the binding, then released Evan's hands. The immediate relief in his upper arms seemed to sap a little more of his strength as his body sagged.

"You will walk." The man's voice had such an unusual accent, making it hard to place either his age or nationality. Definitely young, though.

How humbling. Here he was, Evan MacManus, former captain in the American army and now a trusted spy commissioned by President Madison himself, brought down by a lad with a bow and arrow.

Evan struggled to his feet, spreading them wide to keep from toppling over as his vision swam. Even with his eyes squeezed tight, his body wobbled more than he could control. He shouldn't be this affected by a simple wound, even with the blood loss. Had the arrowhead been tainted? He'd heard tales of Indians dipping the tips in poison before battle.

A hand gripped his arm, giving him something to brace against—until it yanked him forward. Still, the hold kept him upright as he forced one foot in front of the other. The grip felt small, even through the layers of his coat.

Evan forced his eyes open, but the sunlight made the dizziness more intense. He tried squinting, which helped. He had to stay alert, watch his surroundings if he was going to get out of this alive. So far, they appeared to be walking the same path north he'd been riding. Toward the opening between the mountains.

When they reached the spot, his captor loosed a piercing whistle. Evan fought to keep from cringing at the surprise blast so near his ear, but a fresh blade of pain pierced his middle anyway. When a second shrill whistle came, he almost jabbed the lad with his elbow.

But the reply that sounded from the other side of the rock grabbed his focus. They wove around a boulder to proceed through the opening, and Evan squinted again now that he could see bright daylight on the other side.

The place looked to be a meadow of sorts. With figures darting through the winter brown grass. Voices called, or maybe laughed. Children's voices? The pain and blood loss must be making him daft. Or maybe he was being taken to an Indian village. He had to stay awake and watch for a chance to escape.

His captor pushed him forward as other figures approached. These, too, were wrapped in animal skins, but their bulk proved them to be full-grown men. His vision blurred further, even when he tried to focus. He couldn't make out much more than dark or light hair.

Low murmurings sounded around him, yet they seemed to come from so far away. Or maybe it was he who had moved. He had to recover his strength. Squinting again, he tried to straighten. "Who are you?"

The talking around him ceased, and a figure stepped in front of him. He blinked to focus, and the fur cloaking the person began to look familiar. His captor.

The man reached up and pushed the hood off his head, revealing dark hair and a smooth face.

Evan blinked. He must be dafter than he realized, although with the person less than a stride away, it was hard to miss what his eyes took in.

A woman?

Even through his shadowy vision, he could make out the delicate angles of her face. Those piercing dark eyes.

"You have come to Laurent. Now you will tell us why."

The lilt in her voice sounded different now that he could see her. With her tone so melodic, how could he not have recognized her as female?

A fresh wave of dizziness washed over him, and he braced his feet. A hand gripped his arm, that same small hand as before.

"Your purpose, monsieur. Before you swoon, if you please."

Even if he wanted to tell her, his mouth had turned to cotton. Blackness circled the edge of his vision, increasing until he could only see her blurry form through a small hole, like he was looking through a field glass. This lightness in his head almost took over completely. His body sank like it weighed twice as much as usual.

Lord, don't let them kill me. Not yet.

He had too much to make up for. Too much left to fix before he faced the final judgment.

Sign Up for Misty's Newsletter

Keep up to date with Misty's latest news on book releases and events by signing up for her email list at the link below.

MistyMBeller.com

FOLLOW MISTY ON SOCIAL MEDIA

Misty M. Beller, Author   @MistyMBeller

More from Misty M. Beller

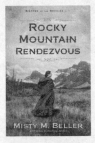

Juniper Collins and her sisters travel west to find the Peigan Blackfoot woman their late father credits with saving his life. Riley Turner became a trapper in the Rocky Mountains to find peace and quiet, but he feels compelled to help the sisters on their mission. But they face more questions than answers as unlikely allies—and enemies—stand in their way.

Rocky Mountain Rendezvous
SISTERS OF THE ROCKIES #1

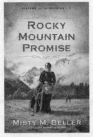

When Lorelei Collins rescues a rare white orphaned buffalo calf, she unwittingly brings people to her Rocky Mountain ranch. When the attention turns threatening, she approaches the mysterious new trading post owner with a proposition, but they are soon faced with a greater threat—one that will test their limits and the love growing between them.

Rocky Mountain Promise
SISTERS OF THE ROCKIES #2

On assignment to help America win the War of 1812, Evan MacManus is taken prisoner by Brielle Durand—the key defender of her people's secret French settlement in the Canadian Rocky Mountains. But when his mission becomes at odds with his growing appreciation of Brielle and the villagers, does he dare take a risk on the path his heart tells him is right?

A Warrior's Heart
BRIDES OF LAURENT #1

◈ BETHANY HOUSE